Venetian Gold

Rachele Modiano Mendes - The early years
Book 3

Silvano Stagni

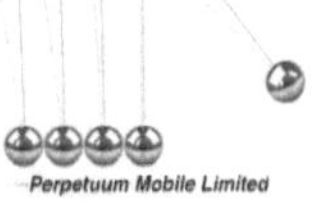

Perpetuum Mobile Limited

 Formatted with Vellum

To Venice, a city that has always been unique. Even before it became a theme park.

Also by Silvano Stagni

Unconditional

A collection of feel good short stories about acceptance, love, and memories.

The Dressmaker's Parcels

The story of the Modiano Mendes clan during Mussolini's racial laws, World War II, and the Holocaust. Spoiler: Rachele and her eldest daughter Emma join the resistance.

From the series: Rachele Mendes Modiano - the early years

Book 1 : **Reflections in the Water**

1921. Rachele Modiano starts working for a Venetian law firm after she married Gabriele Mendes. Her first case turns into a web of fraud, blackmail, and possibly murder. Rachele must protect her client's name and win over a magistrate who dismisses her as an aristocrat toying with the law as a hobby.

Book 2: **Villa Kalman's Secrets**

Venice 1925. Somebody shoots at two teenagers who jumped a fence to retrieve a ball from Villa Kalman's garden. A couple of months later, a young man is found severely beaten and unconscious in the shed of the same villa. Who fired the shot? Who was the young man? Why was he beaten unconscious? Were those events related?

From the series: Rachele Mendes Modiano Investigates

Book 1: **Elena's Memory**

Venice, 1947. The search for the legitimate heir to a couple who did not survive the camps brings a young woman who lost her memory to Venice. The love and support of the extended Modiano-Mendes clan helps her recover her memory. They soon realise that the attempts to get rid of her had nothing to do with the inheritance.

Book 2: **Murders and Masterpieces – A Venetian Mystery**

Venice1866, a Frenchman on his honeymoon, sees an artist sketching a scene. When he visits his workshop, he falls in love with the painting and commissions five versions: one for himself, one each for his two siblings, one for his parents, and another small one as a sample to show them while waiting for the others to arrive.

Venice 1950. Somebody kills an art dealer using one piece of a frame removed from one of the five versions he had in his gallery for sale. Who did it? Why did he take out one side of a frame? A few days later, somebody breaks into the warehouse of an auction house, where another of the five versions is waiting to be auctioned, and removes the left side of the frame. Who broke in? What were they looking for? Is there something hidden in the frame?

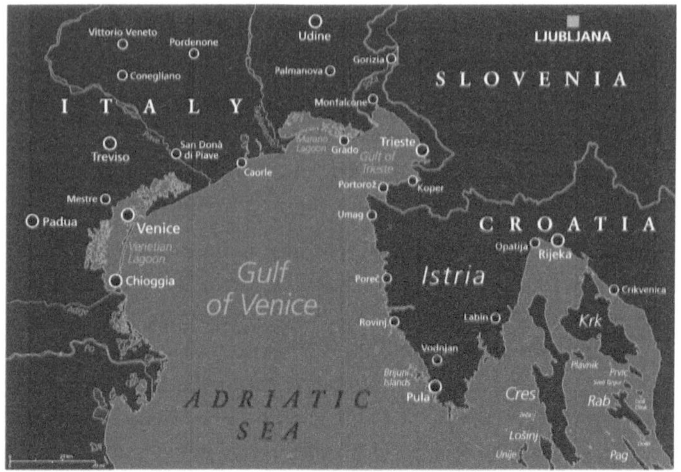

Map of Northeast Italy that includes the locations mentioned in the
book: Venice, Trieste (Triest), Gorizia (Görz), and Monfalcone

Foreword and Cast of Characters

Each series has repeated characters. Five families feature in the series. As time goes by, children are born and family members are lost because they move away or die. Here are the five families at the beginning of the story, in 1929.

Gabriele Mendes, Paolo Mondani, and Alvise Cantoni met in primary school when they were 6 and have been friends ever since. Paolo Mondani was 'emotionally adopted' by the Mendeses after his parents died. Arrigo thinks of Samuele and Fiamma as his grandparents and the Mendes siblings as his uncles and aunt.

The Mendes family from Venice

Samuele Mendes (born 1870), **Fiamma Andrade** (born 1873) – married in 1894

Children and grandchildren mentioned in this book (3 out of 6 children, 4 grandchildren)

- **Carlo Mendes** (born 1923), grandson (son of Raffaele Mendes, the eldest sibling)
- **Gabriele Mendes** (born 1897), married to **Rachele Modiano**
  - **Emma Mendes** (born 1924)
  - **Anna Mendes** (Born 1926)
  - **Diana Mendes** (Born 1929)
- **Myriam Mendes** (born 1905), marries **Michele Bolaffi**
- **Roberto Mendes** (born 1913)

The Modiano family from Trieste

Baron Davide Modiano (born 1860) married to **Esther Coronel** (born 1866)

Children mentioned in this book (3 out of 8)

- **Greta Modiano** (b. 1885)
- **Daniele Modiano** (born 1891), married to **Perla Oppenheim**

The Pesaro de Bonfili family

Count Victor Pesaro De Bonfili (born 1865), **Deborah Camerini** (born 1873) – married in 1900

- **Giorgio Pesaro De Bonfili** (born 1902)
- **Sarah Pesaro De Bonfili** (born 1905)

The Cantoni Family

Alvise Cantoni – (born in 1897), married to **Viola Luzzato** (born in 1899)

- **Franco** (born in 1924)

The Mondani Family

Paolo Mondani – (born in 1897) married to **Sofia Taiman** (born in 1899)

- **Arrigo** (born in 1918)

Other recurring characters

Anita Torgnon – Gabriele and Rachele's live-in housekeeper and Rachele's close friend and confidante. She is considered an integral part of the Mendes family and is always included in family events.

Franco Venier – Lead partner of the Venier-Zanin law firm, Rachele's boss

Dario Zago – At the beginning of the story he is a researcher, then he graduates and, at the end, he is a trainee lawyer.

Carlo Kovach – Former assistant concierge at Pensione Vivaldi, replaces Dario Zago as the researcher for the Venier-Zanin law firm

Antonio Penzo – Judge tasked to supervise police investigations, a friend of Franco Venier and an admirer of Rachele's Professional Skills.

Other characters

Enrico Fonda – The director of a shipping company

Anna Maria Fonda – His Sister

Karl Schweitzer – A Swiss police inspector

Franz Sedlak – A friend of Daniele Modiano (mentioned)

Graf Von Falkenberg – An eccentric German aristocrat.

Chapter One

October 1929 to Early January 1930

Wednesday, 13 November 1929

Franco Venier, one of the two senior partners of the Venier-Zanin law firm, had been reviewing a contract all morning. The Italian translation had something that did not convince him. Unfortunately, the original was in German. He was not fluent in German, and Rachele Modiano Mendes, the senior lawyer who could have read the original, was on leave of absence at home after giving birth. His mind went back to the first-ever conversation they had. He was proud she had made a name for herself in the Venetian legal world, and his peers had stopped teasing him and his partner, Giovanni Zanin, because they had hired a solicitor who happened to be a woman (as Rachele loved to describe herself).

Thinking of Rachele made him decide to call her husband, Gabriele Mendes. He dialled his office number and asked to be put through to him.

"Good Morning, Gabriele, how are you? How are your ladies?"

Gabriele sounded remarkably alert for a father of a three-month-old baby.

"I am fine. The ladies are all fine. Diana has settled in pretty quickly, and she has already dropped the night feed, so we sleep through the night. Emma is busy playing the eldest sister, and Anna has decided that her doll is her daughter and copies everything Rachele does with Diana. Anita has even made a few pretend nappies for her."

"How sweet of Anna. I am impressed you sleep at night. None of my children settled that early. I used to sleep at my parents' before a day in court. Anyway, how's Rachele? Do you think I could ask her to look at a contract in German?"

Franco couldn't see Gabriele's grin.

"Rachele is starting to get bored. If it is not urgent, she would welcome a distraction."

"Perfect! When is a good time to visit? I don't want to interfere with a holiday or a family reunion."

"Rachele's parents are here very often. I like them, and we get along, so it's not a problem. Pick a day between Monday and Thursday, and it should be fine. Friday is the usual bedlam."

"Do you think I could come tomorrow afternoon? Would I wake up the baby if I ring the bell?"

"Tomorrow afternoon should be fine; if it is not, either Anita or I will call you tomorrow morning. Don't worry about ringing the bell. Diana doesn't wake up that easily."

"Lucky you. A feather falling on the floor would have woken up any of my three children when they were babies."

Franco closed the conversation, asked Gabriele to send his best to all the Modianos and the Mendeses he had met. He would be at their home at 4 pm unless someone told him otherwise in the morning.

Thursday, 14 November 1929

Franco Venier arrived at the Mendeses' just when Fiamma (Gabriele's mother), Esther (Rachele's mother), and Aunt Deborah were going to take Emma and Anna, the two older daughters, out shopping. Anita, the housekeeper and the very cherished third adult in the Mendes household, showed him to the sitting room, where the grandmothers and the great-aunt were waiting for Emma and Anna to get ready. He had met them before, when he attended the girls' naming ceremonies.

Deborah Camerini was holding Diana. The two grandmothers had already taken their turn; Franco could not kiss her hand, so he bowed his head instead. He did the same with the other two ladies. Anita asked him if he would like some tea or something else; when he said that tea was fine, Esther Coronel poured him a cup while Anita went to check if Rachele had already sorted out her daughters.

Less than ten minutes later, Rachele emerged with Emma and Anna. Emma, who was almost six, went to Franco Venier and shook his hand.

"Good afternoon, Avvocato[i] Venier, nice to see you again."

The three grand dames looked at her with pride. Anna, a four-year-old who would never allow herself to be outdone by her older sister, repeated Emma's words but forgot to shake his hand. Rachele greeted her boss and took Diana from the Countess, who stood up. They were ready to go.

"As Emma said, very nice to see you again, Avvocato Venier. Apologies for leaving so soon after you arrived, but we are off on a shopping expedition. The grandmothers have decided to buy coats for Emma and Anna, and I decided to tag along."

She then led her two friends and their granddaughters to the door, followed by Anita. Rachele put Diana in the playpen and turned to her boss,

"I hope they will only buy the two coats as promised. Emma and Anna have enough clothes. I shall be surprised if they do. I just hope they don't need a porter; the three of them together are a force of nature. When Anita comes back, we'll move to the study."

Franco Venier smiled. They began discussing the office; Anita came back after seeing everybody out.

"I hope they do not have to hire a porter by the time they are done."

Rachele laughed and turned to her boss.

"What did I just tell you? Come with me to the study."

Once they were in the study, Rachele offered her boss more adult refreshments from her and Gabriele's secret stocks, and then they sat down. Franco Venier took out a folder from his briefcase and handed it over.

"I have a problem with a Swiss contract written in German. Our client is not convinced that the Italian translation makes sense, and he has requested that we review it before he signs. It is an agreement for a bridging loan, and there is no requirement to deliver any materials for the project. You are fluent in

German. Can you check for any inconsistencies between the German and the Italian versions?"

Rachele took the folder from her boss without opening it.

"Who is the client, and how long do I have?"

Franco was surprised at how pleased Rachele was to discuss work. He thought she would still be recovering from the delivery. After all, Diana was three months old, and Rachele was on her leave of absence. Rachele did not miss his quizzical look.

"I will only look at it in between breastfeeding and other things, but I welcome the opportunity to think of something other than nappies, manage sibling rivalries, breastfeeding schedule, etc. When Diana sleeps and Emma and Anna are in kindergarten, I get bored."

Franco Venier closed his briefcase, took a sip of the brandy Rachele had poured him before she sat down.

"That's what Gabriele told me when I called him. Before you're annoyed that I called him first, remember I'm accustomed to my wife, who took a long time to recover from the births of our second and third children. Do you think you'll manage in four weeks?"

Rachele laughed

"I can do it in two. Thank you for this. I needed it. I am still housebound."

They discussed the office for ten to fifteen minutes, then Franco Venier thanked her and told her he had to leave. Rachele saw him out and went back into the sitting room to see if she could extract Diana from Anita's arms.

. . .

09 December 1929

Rachele and Anita had walked Anna and Emma to nursery school. Anita helped Rachele carry the pram with Diana up and down the steps, each time there was a bridge to cross. The conversation between them was about lunch, dinner, and what Anita had to buy at the market. Rachele was on her way to the Venier-Zanin law firm to introduce Diana to her co-workers and discuss the Swiss contract her boss had asked her to review. Anita had offered to walk with Rachele to the law firm, but her friend (and employer) declined her offer. Diana was her third child; she had already coped with prams in Venice twice. Diana was not very heavy; she could manage. Once they had parted company, Rachele smiled at the thought that the smell of the fish market was not nauseous anymore. As she was navigating the Rialto Bridge with the pushchair, she realised how much she missed work. She loved her daughters, but she was looking forward to going back to work in January. It was a great way to start 1930. When she rang the doorbell, the door did not open immediately, then Alvise Cantoni, her colleague and Gabriele's friend since primary school, appeared to carry the pushchair up the flights of steps leading to the Office.

When they reached the first floor, Rachele was welcomed by receptionists and secretaries who all wanted to have a glimpse of Diana. When Franco Venier appeared, they all returned to their desks, except one young typist who was holding Diana, making funny faces, hoping to get a smile. Diana would not stop looking for her mother's face. Franco Venier noticed it and asked the typist to join them in the meeting room and hold Diana in a way she could see her mother. Once they were settled in the meeting room, Franco Venier started paying attention to Diana. The typist noticed that Rachele was the one most eager to start with the business side of the meeting.

"This is a bridging loan, so your client was right to have doubts about clause 15."

Franco Venier's attention was focused on Diana.

"What is clause 15?"

"The one that says that they have to use Fonda Trasporti for all their freight forwarding requirements during the life of the contract."

Franco Venier stopped paying attention to Diana and focused on what Rachele was saying.

"So, it is not a bad translation."

"It is, because the German text is far stricter than the Italian version. You could interpret the Italian translation as regarding all the shipping requirements associated with the contract, since it is a bridging loan, there are none. On the other hand, the German text is clear: Fonda Trasporti, head-quartered in Monfalcone, must handle all shipping requirements."

Franco Venier stood up to pick up a notepad from the top of a cupboard.

"Any other clause in the contract where the translation could lead to a different interpretation?"

"None, I have prepared a page with my notes. I am convinced that if our client signs this contract, he will be required to use Fonda Trasporti until the bridging loan is repaid. Did your client ask why the Milan office of Neue Zugkredit insisted on using a contract in German?"

Franco Venier smiled; he could answer that.

"They claim the head office wanted to ensure all the offices would follow the same way of doing business. Neue Zugkredit mainly deals with project finance contracts."

Rachele was reviewing her notes, searching for something. She did not lift her head to speak.

"This is strange, the contract is for an eight-month bridging loan, with all the clauses you would expect from a bridging loan except clause 15."

Franco Venier did not have an answer to that.

"Thank you for your help. I think I'll suggest a meeting between our client and Neue Zugkredit in Milan to see if we can clarify this inconsistency."

The meeting was over, and Rachele put away her notes, taking Diana from the typist, who was happy that the baby kept looking at her and not at her mother. She put her back in the pram. Franco Venier carried the pram down the stairs; when they reached the ground floor, he thanked Rachele and told her he would call to make arrangements to visit with his wife.

On the way home, Rachele thought she was definitely ready to return to work in January. She loved her daughters, but she was most definitely not a stay-at-home mum.

Tuesday, 07 January 1930

There was excitement in the Mendes household. Emma and Anna were going back to nursery school after the holidays, and Rachele was going back to work after taking time off for Diana's birth. Anita smiled when she entered the kitchen. Rachele had been baking, a sign she felt restless or nervous.

"I did not expect to see you baking this morning. You can't possibly be in court on your first day back to work."

Rachele barely lifted her head. She was focused on placing the raw biscuits on an oven tray.

"It is an important morning. Emma and Anna's nursery starts, and I go back to work. I think I have organised everything."

A timer pinged.

"Please, Anita, take the pastries I prepared for our breakfast out of the oven."

Anita put down the jar of coffee and complied. She had just placed the tray on the cooling rack when Gabriele walked in with Emma and Anna.

"Good morning. The smell of freshly baked croissants is a wonderful way to start the day. What do we need to thank for this surprise?"

Rachele had just finished sorting out the tray of biscuits. Anita was sorting out the children's breakfast, and Gabriele started making coffee. Anita replied as she took the children's mugs and saucers out of the cupboard.

"Rachele's going back to work, and Emma and Anna are going back to nursery."

It had been a busy morning. The whole family left together. Anita pushed the pram with Diana; Emma and Anna walked alongside it, each holding on to their side of the pram with one hand. At the corner with Calle Colombo, Gabriele and Rachele hugged and kissed Emma and Anna, wishing them a good day at their nursery, then they turned right to walk towards their offices.

Gabriele and Rachele loved walking together around Venice. Those walks were their private moments. Silence was never heavy between them; they enjoyed the physicality of being next to each other. They walked past a stationery shop. Gabriele stopped to look for something in the window.

"Do you think they have something that might look like one of your folders, only smaller?"

"Why?"

"I noticed Emma is getting into her role of big sister. She plays grown-up; this morning, she was mimicking you as you were putting things in your briefcase. I want to see if they have something that might resemble the folders I am sure you will start taking home. Remind me to stop here on our way home this evening."

Rachele nodded, then they turned into Riva Del Vin. When they were crossing the Rialto Bridge, Rachele wanted her Canaletto Moment and stopped at the top to look at the Grand Canal towards San Marco.

"I have lived in Venice for nine years, but this never gets old."

Gabriele smiled. He loved his city and was proud that his wife shared that love. They had reached the entrance to Rachele's office. Gabriele kissed his wife on the cheek and started walking toward his office. As usual, Rachele looked at her husband for a short while before turning around and climbing the two flights of steps to her office.

Chapter Two

January 1930

11 January 1930

The combined Mendes and Pesaro de Bonfili clans were walking to lunch after synagogue. Fiamma Andrade and Deborah Camerini had been close friends since they were five; both had only brothers and longed for a sister, so they became as close as sisters, a relationship that continued throughout their lives. By 1930, most of the Venetian Jewish community thought of them as one extended family. They were walking in small groups, as usual, heading for the Pesaro De Bonfili residence near the Ca D'Oro. Anita, another honorary member of the clan, was carrying Diana. Roberto Mendes, Gabriele's youngest sibling, and Samuele Mendes, their father, were walking with the children. Gabriele and Rachele were walking side by side; they were so closely connected that they did not need to hold hands. They did not have to worry about their daughters; the family was taking care of all the children. Once they crossed the bridge over Rio Di Noale, Gabriele broke the silence.

"Did your mother tell you when they are supposed to arrive?"

"Sometime tomorrow, they will stay at Uncle Viktor and Aunt Deborah's. They come to dinner tomorrow, with Uncle Viktor, Aunt Deborah, and your parents."

"That is quite a crowd. Can we fit them all?"

"Yes, we can. By the way, you take care of our daughters this evening. Your mother has organised a meeting of the Mendes wives to discuss Myriam's wedding."

"You will lead the group of women that will accompany the bride to the synagogue. We did not do that."

"We got married in Trieste, under the watchful eye of my father, who made sure we followed the Modiano traditions."

Emma and Carlo, their nephew, wanted to show them something and started running towards them, interrupting their conversation.

13 January 1930

Gabriele and Rachele were on their way to work. They had just said their goodbyes to Anita and their daughters. After a short while, Gabriele turned to his wife.

"So, your parents did not just come to Venice to see their granddaughters?"

"My mother did. My father and Uncle Viktor want to talk to me about something. I'll meet them at 10. Last night they kept telling me I'll find out at work, it was not a family matter."

It was the beginning of Rachele's second week back to work. Her desk was relatively clear of folders. She had finished writing the umpteenth letter to one of her clients, confirming that she had now started working after her five-month break, when the receptionist came to tell her that her 10 am meeting had arrived and was waiting for her in the 'Rialto' meeting room.

When she walked into the meeting room, she found her father and Uncle Viktor sitting down, two thick folders between them. They both stood up when they saw her. They were at her home with their wives the previous day, but her daughters were the main attraction; Rachele and Gabriele could have gone out for a walk, and they did - their presence was not missed.

"So, are you ready to tell me why you booked an appointment with me? You know I will have to bill you for this meeting."

Davide Modiano and Viktor Pesaro de Bonfili looked at each other and smiled. Rachele's father took over.

"This is a genuine business meeting. Our companies will pay the bill. Don't worry, your mother and your aunt Deborah will see to that!"

Rachele smiled. She noticed that her uncle had opened one of the two folders.

"It is a complicated story. We had a friend whose family owns a shipyard in Muggia[i]. He is no longer with us, and his son is negotiating a loan to finance a major upgrade project. There is a strange clause in the contract. The original is in German, but there is an Italian translation."

He takes the top folder and hands it to Rachele.

"We need your opinion on the contract and the translation."

Rachele opened the folder and looked at the front page.

"Another client of the firm is negotiating a loan with the same bank. Does the strange clause have anything to do with Fonda Trasporti? Also, what is your connection with the shipyard?"

Rachele's father picked up the second folder and handed it to her.

"Viktor and I may invest in the shipyard once they have completed their modernisation project. This folder has a preliminary arrangement; we would like your opinion on that as well. The project finance loan contract is one of the things we are looking into before we proceed with the purchase of shares in the shipyard."

"Do you have in mind purchasing a controlling amount?"

"Not really, but we want to be able to name a board member."

Count Viktor Pesaro De Bonfili added with a smile.

"Therefore, we are discussing it here rather than talking about it in a family environment. When can you let us know?"

"Uncle Viktor, I know Dad leaves on Wednesday. I don't think I'll be able to have an opinion in time. Can we aim for next Monday? I'll telephone Dad."

Her father and her uncle had no problem with that. They stood up, getting ready to leave. Rachele's father turned to his daughter.

"Your mother and your aunt have invited themselves to lunch. Your mother plans to use your kitchen to cook dinner for everyone. It will be easier for you, and we won't have to leave Anita out."

Rachele smiled. Anita and her mother got along well, but she didn't know whether they could share a kitchen. She silently prayed they could because she had more important things to do than mediate a conflict between cherished family members.

When Rachele arrived back at the office after her lunch break, the receptionist informed her that Franco Venier had already arrived and was in his office with Dario Zago. Rachele dropped by her office to leave her coat and her handbag and collect the notepad she had used during the morning meeting with her father and her uncle. Her boss had kept the door open. He was not having a confidential conversation with Dario. Franco Venier noticed her and smiled.

"Good Afternoon, Rachele, how was lunch? I was talking to Dario about his future in the firm once he has graduated and passed his state exam[ii], we shall keep him as a trainee lawyer, and you will be his supervisor."

It also meant a career progression for her. She sat down with the notepad still closed and turned to Zago.

"When do you graduate?"

"In a few weeks, I hope to sit for the state exam in March. I don't want to book it now because I don't want to jinx it."

Franco Venier smiled and took out a notepad from a drawer in his desk.

"I understand, although I do not think you'll have any problems."

He rang reception as Rachele and Dario got up and moved to the meeting table. By the time he joined them, the receptionist had appeared with a bottle of water, three glasses, and was ready to take their orders for refreshments. Rachele took a sip of water before starting a summary.

"When I was still on leave, you asked me to check a contract between the Milan office of Neue Zugkredit and one of our clients. The contract was for a bridging loan, and I could not understand the logic behind the clause that would have required our client to use Fonda Trasporti during the contract's life. This morning, Dad and Uncle Viktor brought me another loan contract. This time, Neue Zugkredit will finance a modernisation project in a shipyard in Muggia. The clause to use Fonda Trasporti for the life of the contract is there as well."

Franco Venier finished taking notes.

"I am surprised that a bridging loan and a project finance loan have the same clause. I wonder if there is a connection. Dario, could you research who owns Fonda Trasporti and see if they have any link with Neue Zugkredit?"

Dario turned to Rachele.

"When do you need the information?"

"I promised I'll give my opinion on the contract in a week."

Franco Venier added

"My client needs to sign the contract for the loan by the end of the month.

Dario was silent for a few minutes.

"I'll see what I can do, but I may not have enough time."

He closed his notepad and looked at Franco Venier, who

nodded. The meeting was technically over, but Franco Venier had something else to discuss with Rachele.

"Dario, you can go now. Rachele, do you have some more time for me? If you'd rather not, we can schedule some time for tomorrow morning."

Rachele had time, and Franco briefed her on a new client.

18 January 1930

That Saturday, Rachele did not join Gabriele and her two older daughters in synagogue; she felt she had to spend the morning with Diana, who, at five months, was responding more and more to her environment. She loved her job and could never spend all her time at home with her children, but she treasured the time she had carved out for them. They had guests for lunch, the families of Gabriele's two oldest friends, Paolo Mondani and Alvise Cantoni. The three of them had known each other since the first day of primary school. Paolo was not Jewish, but was integrated into the Mendes clan.

Later that evening, once their daughters were asleep, Gabriele and Rachele asked Anita to babysit and went out for one of their walks. It was one of those crystal-clear, yet freezing, winter evenings that Rachele loved so much. They started walking towards Rialto; when they reached Campo San Polo, Rachele stopped to look at the sky. After a brief silence, she turned to her husband.

"From where we stand now, Campo San Polo looks like a stage. You can imagine the characters of a Goldoni play appear and start saying their lines."

Gabriele turned to his wife with a huge grin.

"I can see it as well, but I also see a vibrant city, a place that has embraced progress, but where people's lifestyle has not changed so much. We walk everywhere. A campo is still the hub of a neighbourhood where children play, and you know all the regulars, either by name or by sight. We have the best of both worlds, a cosmopolitan city looking outward with all the hustle and bustle, and a series of small quiet villages."

They fell silent. Silence between them always felt intimate; they were walking arm in arm, emotionally warmed by the other's presence. The silence continued until they turned onto Riva del Vin, and the Rialto Bridge came into full view. Then, Gabriele turned to his wife.

"We cross the bridge, stop for your Canaletto moment, then we catch a vaporetto to San Stae and return home."

Chapter Three

January 1930

22 January 1930

Rachele no longer needed to set her alarm clock. Her youngest daughter was as reliable as a Swiss clock. Every morning, Diana would wake her up during the same fifteen-minute interval. Rachele would get up, feed her, change her, and then get dressed. Gabriele would take care of their two older daughters while his wife was in the bathroom. That morning, Rachele did not get dressed but put on her dressing gown and went into the kitchen, where she started making her pistachio cake, trying her best not to make any noise so Anita would not wake up.

She had just laid out the ingredients on the kitchen table when Anita appeared, looked at the display, and smiled.

"Gabriele will be delighted when he sees what you are making, or are you baking for the office?"

Rachele had finished weighing everything she had on the table.

She did not turn towards Anita, who was now making coffee for the grown-ups and warming the milk for Emma and Anna.

"I am baking for us. I need to figure out how to present a situation to my father, Uncle Viktor, and another client in a way that matches my level of concern."

Anita knew better than to ask for more details.

"Is it that bad?"

"It is not bad enough to advise them not to sign the contract. I just need more time to address an unusual clause."

Anita looked at the clock in the kitchen.

"I think you have about forty minutes before mayhem starts. Good luck."

When Gabriele walked into the kitchen with Emma and Anna, Rachele was smiling and about to put the cake in the oven. She had figured out what to say to whom.

It was a foggy day. Once Gabriele and Rachele had said goodbye to Anita and their daughters, they watched them disappear into the fog as they made their way to the nursery school. The fog was not thick; it was enough to make the buildings look as if they were behind a veil, a veil that would lift as they approached them. Gabriele loved Venice in the fog. Rachele was planning her morning, so she ignored the beauty around her. She was walking arm in arm with her husband, guided by what she sensed her husband was doing and by her memory of the route to work.

When they got to the first bridge, Gabriele felt the need to say something.

"I know you are still thinking of whatever made you bake this morning, but we are approaching a bridge. I'd hate if you tripped and I had not warned you."

"Thank you, but I am aware of where we are, almost without paying attention to where we are."

Gabriele smiled.

"Well, you have become a Venetian."

Rachele had figured something out in her head. As they crossed the bridge, she began to look up. Gabriele sensed she was now walking next to him, both in body and mind.

Rachele was talking to her father when Dario Zago knocked at her door. Their business conversation was over; they were talking about family. She pointed Dario to a chair on the other side of her desk while she was closing her conversation with Baron Davide Modiano. Once she hung up, she noticed Dario had his notepad out.

"Before we discuss what I would like you to do, when do you graduate? Do you need time off to work on your dissertation?"

Dario closed his notepad and put it on Rachele's desk.

"I graduate on Monday. I have read and re-read my dissertation. If you wake me up in the middle of the night, I can discuss the issues in transitioning from the Austrian to the Italian legal system at the end of World War I."

Rachele smiled

"I lived through that transition. I promise I won't ask you about it. Have you made any progress in figuring out the connection between Neue Zugkredit and Fonda Trasporti? My father and my uncle, Viktor, are our clients in this matter, but there may also be another client who might be interested. But I need to talk to Franco Venier first."

Dario took out his notes.

"At the moment, I have gone as far as I could without a trip to Milan and another one to Trieste. Do you think your father and your uncle will pay for it?"

Rachele took out a folder.

"I know they will. Before you go, let us know when you have a date for your state exam. We need to find a researcher to replace you."

"Why?"

"Because we hope you'll have better things to do."

Dario closed the notepad and told her he would have a plan later that day; there may be travel expenses. They agreed to meet around 4 pm to discuss Dario's plan. Then Rachele stood up, saying she had to check when she could talk to Franco Venier that day, and walked out of her office with Dario.

Rachele checked if Franco Venier was available that morning, so she knocked at his door, asking if he had half an hour for her. He told her to sit down and tell him what she had in mind.

"I need to pick your brain, and maybe I need to ask your permission to contact one of your clients."

Franco was intrigued by what Rachele had just told him.

"Which one?"

"Do you remember the contract you asked me to check last month? Neue ZugKredit bridging loan?"

"The one with the clause about a freight forwarder we both could not explain?"

"The very one. I need to understand why two different contracts have the same clause. I thought that talking to your client might help."

Franco Venier scratched his head, sat upright, and called the receptionist to ask if someone could bring him a coffee. Rachele declined coffee; she also recognised a delaying tactic. Franco Venier put down the phone.

"I am struggling to find commonalities between a bridging loan and project finance. If it is a standard clause in their template, I wonder why they left it for the bridging loan."

Rachele had the perfect introduction to the question she wanted to ask.

"Do you mind if I get in touch with your client? My father and Uncle Viktor are covering the costs for us to learn more about the relationship between the bank and the freight forwarder. I wonder if your client is interested as well."

The conversation paused for a few minutes when a secretary entered carrying a tray with a cup of coffee, a glass of water, and some biscuits. Franco thanked the secretary, took a sip of coffee, and ate one biscuit.

"They are not as nice as your biscuits. Let me call them and then I'll let you know if they are available to talk to you and if they are interested in finding out more about the reason behind that clause."

Rachele took the first remark as a hint that she should bake a batch of biscuits for the office.

"Let me know what your client says."

She stood up and smiled.

"By the way, I'll bring two boxes of biscuits on Monday. One for the office and one for you."

Franco laughed.

"Thank you. I won't take mine home, I promise."

23 January 1930

When Rachele opened the folder Franco Venier had given her the previous afternoon, she realised that the name of the client sounded familiar. She called her father to find out if she was right. Davide Modiano replied on the first ring. Rachele skipped the usual small talk to get to the point.

"The law firm has another client who is negotiating a contract with the same bank as the one you asked me to check. Franco Venier gave me their file. The name looks familiar. Do you do business with Ascanio Moratti's company?"

"I think my father started working with his father. They have been importing jute from Asia for at least 80 years. When Ascanio Moratti, the grandfather of the current owner, Giovanni Moratti, started, he was importing bags from London. Now they import jute from somewhere in Asia and make their bags."

"Did you recommend our firm to them? I understand they are a relatively new client."

Rachele could not see his father's smile, but she had guessed it from the tone of his voice.

"Giovanni asked me if I knew a good law firm; I did not mention that you work there. I assume you can't tell me what the contract is about."

This time, Rachele was smiling.

"No, Dad, I cannot tell you. Thank you. It will be easier for me to ring him. Does he know I am a lawyer?"

Davide Modiano's voice was full of pride.

"I am not sure, but he knows my daughters are all exceptional individuals. I do not think he will be surprised."

Rachele thanked her father and added the information to the page she had prepared, ensuring she had all the important details available when she spoke with Giovanni Moratti.

It turned out that Giovanni Moratti was also a friend of Count Viktor Pesaro De Bonfili. Rachele had no problem establishing her credentials. He knew so much about her family that it was almost as if she were talking to a relative. Rachele had to remember to keep things professional more than once. In the end, she got the information she wanted and secured an agreement to share the costs of Dario Zago's investigation. Giovanni Moratti agreed to request an extension of the deadline to sign the contract by two weeks, giving Dario more time to determine the connection between the bank and Fonda Trasporti.

When Dario arrived with his plan, Rachele had two clients willing to share the costs. After they discussed it, she had to talk to her boss. She had a folder to return and a plan to share with him. After all, Moratti's company was his client. She was about to get up when Franco Venier knocked on her doorpost, smiling.

"Did you know that Giovanni Moratti knew your father? You looked at the contract. Why didn't you tell me?"

"I did not know who Ascanio Moratti was. When I saw the name of the Ascanio Moratti Import's general manager, Giovanni Moratti, it rang a bell,"

Rachele's boss sat in a chair by Rachele's desk. He was smiling.

"Your father has sent us a few clients. He once told me he doesn't mention you because you don't need his help in attracting clients to the firm, and he is right. So now you have two clients to share the cost of investigating Fonda Trasporti and the relationship with Neue ZugKredit."

Rachele handed him the folder.

"My guts tell me that once we know the relationship between those two companies, we'll find the reason behind the clause in every contract. I don't believe that Neue ZugKredit copies all the standard clauses from one loan contract template irrespective of what the loan is for."

Franco Venier picked up the contract and stood up.

"Your guts may be right, or their legal advisors are poor, and if you fancy trips to Zurich, we may try to win their business."

Chapter Four

January-February 1930

30 January 1930

Gabriele was a true '*Venetian of the water*.'[i] He loved the city and its everyday pace. Summer holidays in the Alps were the only time he spent 'on land'. Rachele had been living in Venice since they got married in June 1921. He was still surprised by what she noticed and what she took for granted. The city's reflections in the water still fascinated her, and she would occasionally stop to admire them. That morning, the light was special; the sun, low on the horizon, created a great contrast with the dark clouds hovering in the sky. The view from the Rialto Bridge was fascinating, and Rachele's *Canaletto moment* lasted longer than usual.

They were earlier than usual because Alvise had asked them to meet him for coffee at a café near the law firm. He wanted their advice about a personal decision he had to make. When Gabriele and Rachele arrived, Alvise was already sitting at a table. He nodded at the waiter, who ordered two coffees on his behalf, then he stood up to greet his friends. While they were waiting for coffee, Alvise told them he had started early morning walks to work out things in his head. He started bumping into a man who did not belong to the usual group of early risers. This man was tall, blond, dressed in white, including a white scarf, a white woolly hat, and a white padded jacket. The first time Alvise saw him, he thought of a ghost, except that the man's comments in German did not seem to have any ghost-like features; from what he gathered, they belonged to living humans, not the undead. Gabriele and Rachele smiled at the idea of Alvise thinking he had seen a ghost while walking along the Giudecca Canal early in the morning.

When Alvise and Rachele walked through reception, Dario Zago was already there, trying to look patient, but not fooling anybody. Rachele asked the receptionist if she had any appointments in the morning. When the receptionist confirmed she had not, she invited Dario to follow her to her office. Luckily, she only thought, "So we get it done and over with," but did not say it. He had started talking before they could sit down. Rachele reminded him she had not fetched her notepad yet.

Once they were both sitting down, Rachele's pad was in front of her. Dario was ready to start.

"I need you to thank your brother, Daniele. He knows someone at the Chamber of Commerce, and his friend was very helpful. He saved our clients the cost of spending three days in Trieste. I rang him to make an appointment, and when I arrived, he had all the relevant documents and yearbooks ready."

Rachele told him she would do it later. She also wanted the name of her brother's friend so she could send a thank-you note. Dario was unsure of the last name, so they agreed she would ask her brother. She was eager to check what he had discovered in Milan and Trieste.

"I think I found the connection between NeueZugkredit and Fonda Trasporti."

Dario paused for effect. Rachele dropped the pen and looked at him.

"And?"

Dario smiled and started drawing a chart.

"An Austrian national living in Switzerland owns quite a few shares of Neue ZugKredit. He also owns a controlling stake in a Trieste-based company called AdriaFinance, which, among other things, owns 30% of Fonda Trasporti. The Fonda Family owns the rest. It gets better."

Rachele stopped taking notes.

"What do you mean, it gets better?"

"Well, AdriaFinance owns a shipping line used by Fonda Trasporti when they need to ship things overseas, and a controlling stake in a real estate developer that might be interested in buying the Muggia shipyard that is negotiating the project finance deal with Neue ZugKredit in Milan."

Rachele asked him to repeat everything so she could ensure her notes were accurate. Dario told her he had prepared a written report. He made photostatic copies of all the sources of information. It was expensive, but he thought they might need them as evidence. Rachele had no problem with the expense.

"When I first met you, I realised you had a good sense of what could or could not be used as evidence. You will be a brilliant lawyer. By the way, when is your exam?"

"I was too late to enrol for February, so, hopefully, I'll be a qualified lawyer from mid-March."

"Does Franco Venier know?"

"Not yet. I plan to tell him once we have finished here."

03 February 1930

It was a lovely day; most of those leaving the Spanish synagogue stopped to look at Diana, some of them trying to coax a smile out of her, attempts that were seldom rewarded with an actual smile. It was Samuele and Fiamma's turn to host the Mendes/Pesaro De Bonfili clan. So, they were all walking towards Campo del Ghetto Novo to cross the second bridge and head to the Mendes residence for lunch. It would typically take 5 to 10 minutes, but on Saturday morning after the Service, it usually took about half an hour. There were many people to talk to, and a baby was a great attraction. Gabriele and Roberto, his youngest brother, were walking alongside Anita, who was pushing the pram with Diana inside. They were getting most of the attention. Rachele was walking with Fiamma and Countess Deborah. Myriam, Gabriele's only sister, was getting married three weeks later, and there were things to organise. Deborah Camerini, Countess Pesaro De Bonfili, had taken over the organisation of the pre-wedding activities. She was explaining her plan, sharing more details than Rachele would have liked to hear.

They were crossing the bridge into Campo del Ghetto Novo. Rachele had every intention of being part of everything the countess was planning. She liked her sister-in-law, and she also liked Gabriele's brothers' wives. It would not have been a problem, unless.

"Do you think it would interfere with Diana's feeding times?"

This time, Fiamma felt she had to answer.

"It shouldn't, but we have already asked Anita if she didn't mind taking care of Diana, just in case."

Rachele excused herself and moved alongside Gabriele, who was talking to Alvise Cantoni and his wife. They were talking about their children, who were walking together as a group, corralled by various members of the clan into moving in the right direction.

By then, they were leaving Campo del Ghetto Novo, crossing the bridge that would lead to Fondamenta del Ghetto Novissimo and ultimately to Gabriele's parents' home. Roberto was making sure that all the children were accounted for and ready to go inside. Gabriele and Alvise spotted Paolo Mondani and his family arriving from their home in Rialto. Emma and Franco Cantoni noticed them as well and started running towards Arrigo, their son, despite Roberto Mendes' protestations.

06 February 1930

Deborah Camerini, Countess Pesaro De Bonfili, had finished a profitable meeting with the owner of Pensione Vivaldi, who had commissioned her to look for four mid-market Venetian landscapes. He was walking her to the door when Carlo Kovach, an assistant concierge, approached them.

"I am sorry to interrupt. Wolfgang Meyer just asked me if we know a lawyer who speaks German. He needs to have a contract checked."

Countess Deborah had a huge grin.

"I know one. Call the Venier-Zanin law firm and ask for our legal advisor, Avvocato Modiano. I think I still have her business card in my handbag. She is fluent in German and very good."

She did not specify that she was referring to her niece, and she usually carried a few of her business cards in her handbag, just in case.

Carlo Kovach thanked her, took her business card, and said he would contact Avvocato Modiano immediately on behalf of their client. The countess smiled, and the small talk with the hotel owner continued until they reached the door. They had to stop because somebody was coming in through the revolving door.

The countess couldn't help but notice the eccentric man who had just come in; tall, blond, dressed in white, including a white scarf, a white woolly hat, and a white padded jacket. Her client noticed her reaction.

"He is Graf Wilhelm von Falkenberg, a German-born aristocrat from Zurich, a regular client. He likes to dress in white."

"If I had seen him around at night, I would have wondered for a few seconds whether I had seen a ghost."

That comment made her client smile.

"I understand. I think my wife had the same reaction the first time we saw him."

While Countess Deborah was reacting to the unusual guest, Carlo Kovach rang the number on the business card to arrange an appointment with Avvocato Modiano on behalf of Mr Meyer for the following Monday, February 10th, at 11:00 a.m. Carlo wrote the directions to the law firm, thanked the secretary who had taken the call, and then marked the location on a map of the Rialto Bridge area.

10 February 1930

Rachele had mixed feelings about Mondays. Weekends were short enough for her to enjoy time with her daughters and the rest of the family, but they were long enough to welcome being at her desk. She loved her daughters and made a point of spending as much time as possible with them, but she also loved adult interaction. She felt lucky to have the support of Anita, her mother-in-law, and her entire family. They were the ones who made it all possible.

She was sipping coffee, thinking of what she had to bake for the forthcoming mega-birthday party. Her two older daughters, Emma and Anna, were born in February. They were exactly two years and two days apart, so traditionally they had one big birthday party for both of them.

Dario Zago knocked at her door; he was already transitioning from mere research to basic legal work.

"I am reviewing this contract; can you help me understand how it is possible that two clauses contradict each other?"

Rachele took the contract.

"You need to figure out what the two clauses mean, what protection they give to Count Pesaro De Bonfili or its supplier..."

A secretary interrupted her.

"Excuse me, Avvocato Modiano, your 11 o'clock appointment has arrived and is waiting in the Rialto meeting room."

Rachele took her notepad and stood up.

"Thank you. Please bring me a folder for new clients in about half an hour. Dario, I will come and look for you once I have finished; if it is too late, we'll talk immediately after our lunch break."

When Wolfgang Meyer heard the door open, he stood up and greeted Rachele in very formal German. Rachele had never been called 'Frau Rechtsanwältin'[ii]. She hoped she did not show her surprise, was equally formal, asking her visitor how she could help.

"I need you to review a contract in German before you organise a translation into Italian. There is a clause I don't understand."

The choice of words puzzled Rachele.

"What is the contract for?"

"I run a company based near Zurich. We manufacture small precision equipment and supply a watch company on Giudecca Island, as well as two companies based on the mainland near Venice. We often negotiate large contracts for deliveries across six months to a year. I thought we could have an agreement with a bank in Switzerland to organise finance for those large contracts."

"Why do you need to translate the contract into Italian? You and the bank are both German-Swiss."

"Well, Neue ZugKredit, that is the name of the bank, wants the client to countersign each contract, confirming the order they are funding. However, regardless of the translation, there is a clause in the original German template that I do not understand. I need you to explain it to me."

"I promise you, this is the last question, and then I am ready to answer yours. Why did you look for a lawyer in Venice?"

"Because I received the contract the day before leaving Zurich, and I put it in my briefcase to read on the train. There was nothing out of the ordinary until I came to a specific clause. That's why I am here. You came highly recommended. I am leaving tomorrow morning for Trieste to meet with two potential clients. I'll be back on Monday and will spend two weeks in Venice with my wife. It is our wedding anniversary. If you agree to take me as a client, I'll ask the hotel to organise a messenger to deliver the contract."

Rachele wondered why Wolfgang Meyer had not asked questions about her experience or the law firm's rates. Anyway, it was not up to her to explain them.

"Congratulations on your anniversary. Is your Italian good enough to have a conversation about our rates and our terms of engagement?"

Wolfgang Meyer looked more relaxed. He thought his Italian would be good enough. Rachele called the firm's accountant and asked him to come and discuss the terms of engagement, the form, and the down payment. Once the accountant joined them, she excused herself, thanked Wolfgang Meyer for his business, and told the accountant to ring her office if there were any communication issues. Then she apologised once again to her client in very formal German, saying she had something urgent to attend to and left the meeting room.

Chapter Five

February 1930

14 February 1930

Leaving synagogue after a service was always a slow process. There was always somebody you wanted to talk to, somebody you hoped to avoid, and somebody who cornered you, leaving no room for you to escape. Gabriele loved those who exchanged a nod or a wave with him from afar, but did not stop him on his way out. He was the first of his family to reach the designated spot where members of the Mendes clan had gathered since he could remember. Slowly, everybody else arrived, Rachele being one of the last ones.

"I wish I had a coin for every person who asked me what I had done with the daughters."

Countess Deborah and Fiamma were the last ones to join the group. Gabriele kissed both of them. As usual, Gabriele's father, Samuele, and Count Viktor checked that everybody was present and correct before they started walking towards

Gabriele's parents' home for dinner. Gabriele was walking arm in arm with Rachele.

"I am looking forward to an evening with adults. It feels odd that there are no children around. I wonder how Anita and Myriam are doing with all of them having dinner at our place."

"Well, tonight we discuss the last details of Myriam's wedding day. According to your family tradition, the children and the bride are excluded from this conversation, which is why Anita and Myriam are having dinner with all the children. Arrigo wanted to be there as well, so Paolo and Sofia decided to help Anita and find out what they are supposed to do tomorrow afternoon when they come after lunch."

They continued walking in silence, simply enjoying their closeness. It was not a very long walk. It was a clear night with the moon; Gabriele was looking forward to their walk home after dinner.

17 February 1930

Rachele had an easier Monday morning than she expected. The day did not start very well; the entire household overslept, and she and Gabriele did not have their usual relaxed walk to work. They walked as briskly as they could without running, and they did not have time to linger on top of the Rialto Bridge for Rachele's Canaletto moment. She spent the morning revising a contract for her Uncle Viktor and taking notes for the meeting they were supposed to have that afternoon, before negotiating with the other party the following day. The phone interrupted her work; she did not expect to hear from Carlo Kovach, the assistant concierge of Pensione

Vivaldi, who had organised her meeting with Wolfgang Meyer the previous week.

"I am sorry to interrupt your morning, but something happened yesterday after Wolfgang Meyer's wife arrived from Zurich. We have the police here, and a very distressed Frau Meyer would like to talk to a lawyer. The owner has informed me that Pensione Vivaldi will cover the cost of your time. I hope she calms down after talking to you. Her husband is due back from Trieste this evening."

"What happened?"

"She arrived yesterday evening. Everybody was busy, so I took her to her husband's room. However, when I found the door unlocked, I told her to wait in the corridor and went inside. Somebody had ransacked the room. I closed the door, took her back downstairs, then gave her and Mr Meyer a temporary room for two nights, and later called the police. They are here now."

"I can talk to Frau Meyer now. We'll discuss the billing after I have spoken to her and only if it is necessary."

Carlo thanked her and passed the phone to Wolfgang Meyer's wife.

"Good Morning, Frau Rechtsanwältin Modiano, thank you for talking to me. I don't know what happened. How long can the police keep my husband and me away from our room, and is my husband in any trouble? Herr Kovach told me he came to see you."

Rachele tried her best to reassure her.

"The police will give you access to the room when they have finished. It shouldn't take you over 24 hours. Please call me again if you are unable to access the room by tomorrow lunchtime. I cannot discuss the details of my meeting with your husband, but he forgot to send me the contract he wanted me to review. So I can't be of much help."

"I understand, but do you think my husband is in trouble?"

"It looks as if your husband is the victim; that is the only thing I can say. Please, call me again if you need any help or just a sympathetic ear."

She had just finished talking to Frau Meyer when her phone rang again; this time it was Antonio Penzo on the phone. The junior judge had been sceptical of her abilities ten years earlier; now, he was one of her strongest admirers among the Venetian legal professionals.

"Judge Penzo, good morning. What can I do for you?"

"A room at Pensione Vivaldi has been ransacked. We found a contract in German with your business card clipped to it."

"If you are referring to Wolfgang Meyer's room, he is our client. I just spoke to his wife, who arrived from Zurich yesterday; she told me what happened."

Rachele could almost sense the smile on Antonio Penzo's face.

"Do you always find out about things before we do?"

Rachele could not help but laugh.

"Only when it involves a client."

Antonio Penzo had not come to the point yet.

"Can you help me with the contract? It is in German, and our German interpreter is sick."

"I can, but only after I have seen the contract. Wolfgang Meyer forgot to send it to me, as he promised when he came to our offices before his trip to Trieste."

Antonio Penzo told her he would organise a messenger from the police. They agreed to talk at 4 pm, once Rachele could review the contract. After she put the phone down, Rachele wondered whether she should tell Gabriele and Anita that she would work through lunch. She went back to her uncle's contract and decided she would not have to skip lunch after all. She only had two pages left.

When she received Mr Meyer's contract, she almost changed her mind again. It had what she had started to call the 'Fonda Trasporti clause' in it. The rest was an average export finance contract, with the loan intended to enable Mr Meyer's company to extend credit to its Italian clients.

When Antonio Penzo arrived at the law firm, Rachele summarised the contract and then discussed the clause that had puzzled three of their clients so far. They agreed that whoever ransacked the room was after something else, because the contract was on the desk, obvious, and it did not even appear to have been moved. All the drawers were on the floor, their contents spread out throughout the room. Rachele called Dario Zago to explain to the judge the connection between the bank and Fonda Trasporti. They also agreed that she would inform him if they came across any other information relevant to the police investigation, and Antonio Penzo promised to share with her anything that emerged from the inquiry regarding the Swiss Bank or the shipping company.

Her uncle Viktor, Count Pesaro De Bonfili, was the last meeting of her day; he was still there when Gabriele arrived to walk home with her. Count Viktor greeted him warmly.

"Let's all have drinks together. I'll call Deborah."

Rachele was not in the mood.

"Thank you, Uncle Viktor. Unfortunately, we cannot leave Anita to cope with bedtime with no notice, maybe another time."

Gabriele did not want to contradict his wife, but felt that they had time to socialise and go home to share the last hour of their daughters' day. It was only when Rachele's 'Canaletto moment' on top of the Rialto bridge lasted longer than usual that he realised that there was something that was troubling his wife. Perhaps 'troubling' was too strong a concept, but there was something that occupied her thoughts.

"The proverbial penny for your thoughts. What's wrong?"

For a fleeting moment, Rachele looked surprised, then she smiled at her husband.

"Was I that obvious?"

Gabriele smiled and raised his eyebrows. Rachele realised she was, at least to her husband.

"Today, I received a call from a distressed wife. Her husband signed up with us last week. I was wondering how she must have felt arriving at their hotel in Venice and finding her husband's room ransacked. However thoughtful the hotel staff might have been, it must have been a huge shock. Her husband is supposed to be back in Venice this evening. He had gone to Trieste for a business trip."

"Why does she still occupy your thoughts?"

Rachele smiled and shrugged her shoulders.

"I don't know. I know why you are always on my mind. My initial reaction was to ask her if she wanted to have lunch with a friendly face. I realised she had called her husband's lawyer, so I kept it professional, understanding but professional."

Gabriele drew her closer. They started walking arm in arm, and Rachele responded, tightening her grip. They were silent for a while until they walked past a Calle that led to the home of their friends Paolo and Sofia Mondani. Rachele mentioned she might call Sofia to organise something with all the children; Arrigo, their son, loved playing the big brother to their daughters. Gabriele noticed his wife was more relaxed and decided not to mention the conversation she had with her client's wife earlier that day. They will soon be at home and will be inside the Mendes bubble, a perfect end to their day.

18 February 1930

Rachele woke up early, feeling that she was missing something. Baking was her refuge, her way to focus on something else while the back of her mind kept working. Since Diana was born, she hadn't baked as often as she wanted to. That morning, it took her less time to feed Diana, so she started baking. A pistachio pie for her family and biscuits for the office. At some point, she noticed Anita's presence. They worked well together in the kitchen; each one focused on their tasks, but was ready to help the other if needed. Anita started grinding the coffee beans.

"Good morning, Rachele. Is it working?"

"What is working?"

"You bake early in the morning to calm down if you are anxious, or to solve a problem that puzzles your mind. Is baking working?"

Rachele smiled. Her loyal friend and housekeeper knew her well.

"I think so. I have a better idea of what I need to find out."

Gabriele arrived in the kitchen looking for coffee. He noticed Anita grinding the beans and went back to get dressed and wake up Emma and Anna. By the time they entered the kitchen, breakfast was ready.

When she arrived at work, she bumped into Dario Zago coming out of the typists' room.

"Do you have time this morning to go back to Pensione Vivaldi?"

Dario figured out that she had started the conversation in her mind as she was climbing the stairs to the office.

"Good morning, Avvocato Modiano. I'll follow you to your office, where you can take off your coat, and we'll start from the beginning."

Rachele removed the scarf.

"Good morning, Dario, I have done it again, haven't I? My husband would tell me to start from the prologue and not from Chapter 4."

By now, they were in her office. She put her briefcase and handbag on a chair and took off her coat.

"In the past two months, three clients have brought me a contract with an unusual clause involving a company called Fonda Trasporti. Actually, the third client, Wolfgang Meyer, forgot to send me the contract. I found out because Antonio Penzo came to me because the police interpreter is unwell."

She retrieved her handbag and briefcase and moved them to a small table behind her desk, then sat down.

"Anyway, Wolfgang Meyer's room at Pensione Vivaldi was ransacked. I need you to talk to their assistant concierge Carlo Kovach and ask him if he remembers what was on the room's table or dresser, or anything where Mr Meyer could have left the contract lying around."

Dario sat on one of the two armchairs.

"What are we trying to find out?"

"I need to understand why they ransacked the room, and our client's wife told me that Carlo Kovach walked into the room and, when he realised somebody had ransacked it, he stopped her from entering and called the police. I hope he can still tell us what he saw. There is no point in asking to see the room. I assume the police have finished with it and they have tidied up everything."

"What is the connection with Wolfgang Meyer's request to check a contract?"

Rachele had to smile. Dario would be a great asset to the law firm.

"This is something Franco Venier would have said. Anyway, I wonder why he asked to find a German-speaking lawyer in Venice rather than having his legal advisor in Zurich handle it. I just want to ensure that there is nothing that could come back to haunt us if we work with him. Currently, we have taken no action because Judge Penzo showed me the contract, and I only have a vague idea of what he wants to know. So I can just give back his deposit and not take him on as a client."

Dario stood up again.

"I see. Do you want me to go now?"

"It is important to talk to Carlo Kovach as soon as possible, telephone Pensione Vivaldi to check he is there, otherwise you would waste a trip."

Dario realised she was moving on to the next thing in her mind.

Dario Zago arrived at Pensione Vivaldi when the police were leaving. Carlo Kovach informed him that the staff had not yet cleaned Wolfgang Meyer's room, and his wife was out. He can take Dario to see the room and discuss with him what he saw when he entered the room on Sunday evening. He added that his shift will end in an hour. Dario suggests they go to the law firm once they are done, so he can talk to Avvocato Modiano and ask questions.

On the way to the room, they met a tall, blond-haired man completely dressed in white. Carlo greets him in German; Dario looks uncomfortable. He feels he has seen a ghost. Carlo smiles.

"Graf von Falkenberg is an eccentric regular guest. The first time you see him, he almost looks like a ghost. He always wears white. His pale complexion and light blond hair make him look ghostly, especially in dimly lit places like hallways.

Dario smiles uncomfortably.

"I wondered whether I saw a ghost. I see the police left the door open. Let's inspect the room."

Carlo Kovach, Rachele, and Dario were in a meeting room. Carlo was telling her what he remembered from the previous Sunday evening.

"I approached the door holding the second key; I would have opened the door and then let Frau Meyer in. When I put the key in the lock, I realised the door was open. So, I put down Frau Meyer's suitcase, told her to wait, and went in; I saw drawers on the floor and their contents everywhere."

He closed his eyes.

"The room has a desk to the right of the window. They had removed all the drawers, but the desk still looked tidy. I was worried that someone might still be in the room, so I didn't notice what was on the desk. I opened the wardrobe, inspected the bathroom, and then left the room. Told Frau Meyer I would find another room for her for a couple of nights because I had to call the police. Then I gave her the only room we had available, a suite."

Rachele had been taking notes; she thanked Carlo and looked at Dario, telling him it was his turn to speak.

"I saw the room after the police had been there for a day and a half, so any evidence is contaminated. However, I noticed that all the surfaces were tidy, as if nobody had touched them. However, they seem to have looked behind the two framed pictures in the room."

Carlo intervened

"They might have looked for a safe. Our rooms do not have a safe, so we request that our guests leave their valuables with us. We have a room with a lot of safety boxes of various sizes."

Dario had not finished.

"I found a small door on the wall by the left bedside table. The wallpaper almost hid it. A tiny thread had been broken; somebody had found it and opened it. So I opened it. The inside was small and empty."

Again, Carlo intervened.

"That used to have the bell to summon staff. We replaced them with in-room telephones last year. I think we are one of the few establishments at our level with in-room phones. All the top hotels have them."

Rachele stopped taking notes.

"So, we cannot know whether the police found it, opened it, and took the content, or those who ransacked the room found it and took the content..."

Carlo Kovach interrupted her.

"...or if Herr Mayer hid something sensitive in there and then took it when he left for Trieste. He has been a regular guest for years. He would have known where the bell used to be."

Dario was expecting Rachele's reaction. He knew she hated being interrupted. Rachele controlled herself. After all, she had just met Carlo Kovach.

"Did you see Herr Meyer leave on Sunday?"

Carlo took out a diary.

"I did. I called Matteo Masiero, his usual taxi driver. By the way, the same driver will meet him at the station when he arrives from Trieste."

"Did you feel that Herr Meyer left in a hurry, or was he worried?"

"He leaves early, allowing more than enough time to catch the train. I did not think he looked concerned or tense."

Rachele closed her notepad. Thanked Carlo Kovach for his time and his co-operation, asked Dario to see him out, and went back to the office. When Dario returned, she saw she was in her 'thinking pose', with eyes closed, her hands joined, and her nose 'resting' on the two index fingers. He sat down and waited a few minutes before coughing. Rachele opened her eyes and sat up straight.

"Based on what I heard, the reason they ransacked the room has nothing to do with the contract. It could be something opportunistic, such as forgetting to close the door. What do you think?"

Dario waited a few seconds before answering.

"I am very much aware that I have seen the room after the police had been, but based on what Carlo Kovach told me and on a couple of details I saw, it was not random. Whoever did it was looking for something. It wasn't the contract."

"What makes you say that?"

"The drawers in the bedside tables were not on the floor. I doubt the police put them back. The police inspection of the room could explain the state of the wardrobe. The little cubbyhole where the buzzer used to be is also interesting. Don't ask me why, but I think somebody used it to hide something and put a hair or a thread to check whether somebody else opened it."

Rachele was silent for a moment.

"Well, we'll reserve judgement until I speak to Wolfgang Meyer. I'll leave him a message to call me. When I speak to him, I will not mention that I have seen the contract. We may not want him as a client."

Chapter Six

February 1930

19 February 1930

When Rachele was baking early in the morning, it meant she needed to be active to calm her worries or set them aside. Anita did not expect to see her working the dough and singing softly.

"Good morning. You are not usually in such a good mood when you bake."

Rachele did not stop kneading the dough.

"That's because I am preparing Emma and Anna's favourite biscuits to take to nursery school for their birthday parties."

Anita started laying out the kitchen table for breakfast while the coffee was brewing.

"When do we bake for the family celebration?"

"I plan to come home early from work and start working on biscuits and cakes for the family party. Myriam and Sofia are coming to help us and stay for dinner. Arrigo will play big brother, and Gabriele will collect Paolo when he comes home from work."

As they were crossing Campo San Giacomo dall'Orio, Emma could not stop talking. She was excited about the birthday party she would have at their nursery school. Anna was holding onto the pushchair, talking to Diana, who, at six months, was looking at her, diverting her attention to Emma whenever her eldest sister's voice grew louder. When Gabriele and Rachele turned right on their way to work, they stayed silent for a while, enjoying peace and quiet. Then Rachele put her hand into Gabriele's coat pocket, tightening the grip on his arm.

"It is very convenient that Emma and Anna's birthdays are two days apart, so I only have one big party to organise. Although we have a small celebration on their actual birthday."

They were crossing the first bridge in their walk towards their professional life. As they were walking down the stairs, Gabriele remarked they were walking along a canal that had been filled in. Rachele's mind was elsewhere.

"Do not forget that this evening I leave the office early, and you need to meet Paolo on your way home. They are having dinner with us."

"I am impressed by how well you are organising everything."

"I am a working mother who must be organised to cover everything without taking much time off or losing too much sleep. However, I wonder how I would manage without Anita.

She is my real secret to balance being a mother with being a lawyer."

Rachele paused; somehow, bridges always marked a change of tone in their conversation. Rachele was silent for a while. When they reached Campo San Polo, she turned to her husband.

"When I was pregnant with Emma, my eldest sister Greta was organising her family's move to Haifa. I asked her how she reconciled being a mother with being a surgeon. She quoted her three pillars: help, organisation, and coffee. At the time, I thought I understood. Now they have become my three pillars as well."

"You and your sisters are all exceptionally strong women. I admire you for that."

"Thank you. I mean it. Most men would not like their wives to work after they had children. I am very lucky you don't have a problem."

"I do not see it as a problem. It is part of who you are."

It was Gabriele's turn to be silent. Once they reached the top of the Rialto Bridge and Rachele had her Canaletto moment, it was Gabriele who tightened the grip.

"I am not sure I'll be able to come home for lunch today. We have our last discussion before the project for the road bridge from the mainland receives the official go-ahead. I'll let you know by 11 o'clock."

"Good luck and don't forget to tell Anita as well."

They kept walking in silence until they reached Rachele's office. Gabriele kissed her on the cheek and started walking towards his office. Rachele stood there looking at him for a short while, shook her head, and went inside.

Rachele had barely settled down in her office when Dario Zago appeared to discuss the contracts. Nobody in the law firm liked the clause forcing the signatory to use Fonda Trasporti for all their freight forwarding needs. Rachele needed to reach a decision. They had been looking into it for over a month.

"I have a meeting with Wolfgang Meyer later today, and one with my father and my uncle Viktor on Monday, also Giovanni Moratti, Franco Venier's client, must sign the contract by the end of the month to have the finance lined up at the right time, they should have signed it already. What do we tell them?"

Dario didn't answer immediately.

"A major shareholder in the bank also has an interest in the company that is a shareholder in Fonda Trasporti. It is a controversial reason to add an unusual clause to the three contracts. I know that my opinion cannot be considered legal advice at the moment."

"That's where you are wrong. Everybody who has reviewed those contracts thinks the clause is perfectly legal; it is just bizarre. We are all trying to figure out why. Your opinion is as good as mine. In a way, it is even better because you are the one who discovered the connection between the bank and Fonda Trasporti."

"This could also be a way to make sure that the same individual makes money out of all his investments."

"That as well, but it is not technically illegal. So, what do you think I should say?"

They discussed it for about ten minutes, then they agreed with the message that it was legal, but very unusual, and they would also disclose the connection between the bank and Fonda Trasporti.

By the time Wolfgang Meyer arrived at the law firm, Rachele was ready. She had worked it out in her head during the walk home for lunch and the walk back to the office afterwards. Her client stood up as she entered the meeting room, carrying her notepad and his contract. After the usual social chit-chat, she came to the point.

"I do not think there is anything problematic with this contract, except one clause. The one about Fonda Trasporti: from the moment you sign the contract, you must use them for all your shipping requirements. The same would apply to any of your clients. Now, there is nothing illegal in that, but in the last two months, we have come across two other loan deals offered by Neue ZugKredit, and they have the same clause."

Wolfgang Meyer took a sip of water.

"I had time in Trieste and I took a side trip to Monfalcone to see Fonda Trasporti. They seemed a perfectly legitimate operation to me."

"I am sure they are, but they appear in three different contracts. One of them is a bridging loan. There is no need to insert that clause; that's why we thought it was odd. Your contract could be the only one where that clause might be relevant."

Rachele was not surprised that her client took his time to comment.

"Did you figure out why the clause is in all the contracts?"

Rachele smiled and took out a drawing from her notepad.

"We asked our researcher to look into any connection between Neue ZugKredit and Fonda Trasporti, and he found an interesting one. If you look at this diagram, you can see that the same person has a direct or indirect interest in both."

Wolfgang Meyer took his time to study the chart.

"Is it the only problematic thing in the contract?"

"Yes, the rest is fairly standard. Provide an Italian translation for your clients, or even better, ask the Milan office of Neue Zugkredit to provide one."

"I checked Fonda Trasporti. My clients may or may not like that clause, but I'll let them negotiate directly with the bank in Milan. Thank you very much for your help. Please send me the bill to the Hotel. I'll be there for two more weeks."

He stood up, and Rachele walked him to reception. Wolfgang Meyer thanked her for her services, and she thanked him for using the Venier-Zanin law firm. On her way back to her desk, she wondered why she had the gut feeling she would see him again soon.

22 February 1930

The entire Mendes/Pesaro De Bonfili clan was walking to Gabriele's parents' home for lunch after synagogue. Rachele's parents were visiting from Trieste for Emma and Anna's birthday party. Also, Baron Davide and Count Viktor had a meeting with Rachele the following Monday.

Rachele was walking alone. Countess Deborah approached her just when they had crossed the bridge into Campo del Ghetto Novo.

"You look like somebody deep in thought. Is everything OK?"

Rachele was deep in thought and was surprised somebody spoke to her.

"I was looking at my mother and my mother-in-law walking arm in arm and talking; I was wondering what the two grand-mothers are plotting for tomorrow."

Countess Deborah could not resist a smile. She knew what they were plotting.

"You are forgetting great-Aunt Deborah as a possible co-conspirator."

Rachele did not know whether to smile or be concerned, so she chose to smile.

"I don't want to know. Plausible deniability is my way of life."

The Countess started talking about people they saw in syna-gogue. Rachele seldom started gossiping, but once somebody else started, she enjoyed it for a while. Once they crossed the bridge into the Fondamenta leading to the Mendes home, Deborah changed the subject.

"I know you do not want to discuss work on Shabbat, but technically, this is family, not work. This morning at breakfast, I overheard my husband and your father talk about Daniele. He is very worried that his friend may lose the shipyard."

"Thank you for letting me know. I don't think it has any connection to work, but I understand my brother may be worried. I might telephone him when we are back home after Shabbat."

Chapter Seven

February 1930

24 February 1930

It was the morning after the big joint birthday party. They had hosted many family and friends of Emma and Anna, as well as their parents. Luckily, the weather was nice, and the children played in the campo after they had the birthday cake and biscuits.

On their way to work, Gabriele and Rachele were still talking about the party and how happy Emma and Anna were to be at the centre of the attention. The day was foggy; they felt the caigo[i] wrapped around them like a blanket. Everybody was enveloped in their coats and scarves, and was busy going wherever they had to go. It was very intimate. They walked in silence, arm in arm, enjoying their closeness until they reached the bridge over Rio De Le Do Torre (Canal of the two towers), where Gabriele asked Rachele what she had been discussing with her parents when they had disappeared into the study for half an hour. Rachele stopped walking.

"On Shabbat, Aunt Deborah told me she had overheard a conversation between my father and Uncle Viktor. They are trying to help Daniele's closest friend, Franz Sedlak, keep the shipyard he and his siblings have inherited from their father. I wanted to discuss the personal side outside the office. Today I have a meeting with Uncle Viktor and my father. I assume we shall discuss the business side."

They started walking again; their silence lasted until they turned onto Riva del Vin and came into full sight of the Rialto Bridge. Gabriele had been thinking about his brother-in-law.

"Why is Daniele worried?"

"Franz Sedlak is for him what Paolo and Alvise are for you. Of course, he is worried; he also feels there must be something he can do. I will call him when I am at my desk, before I start my day."

"I wish I knew more about your siblings' lives. I would like to do anything practical to help or support them. I enjoy being around your family, but the opportunities to spend time with them are few and far between. We should see them more often, either here or in Trieste."

Rachele smiled and tightened her grip on her husband's arm. They had now reached the Rialto Bridge, and they stopped for Rachele's usual Canaletto moment. Then they switched to discussing the practicalities of the day. When they reached Rachele's office, Gabriele kissed her on the cheeks, then lingered a bit, watching her climb the stairs before turning back and walking to his office.

Rachele was looking at her notes. When she spoke to her brother, the supportive sister became the family's legal advisor; she offered Daniele some suggestions for his friend Franz. The meeting with her father and her Uncle Viktor added to the notes she had taken during the phone call. Her instinct was telling her that there was something not quite transparent in the relationship between Fonda Trasporti and Neue Zugkredit; she was looking at Dario Zago's diagram, hoping to find an answer there. She wondered if somebody could fund Dario's time in finding out more about the individual who owned shares in the Swiss bank and had an indirect stake in the freight forwarder. As far as Franz Sedlak was concerned, she had little time. He had to sign the contract by mid-March or lose the loan. The Milan office of the bank was aware that Baron Davide Morpurgo and Count Viktor Pesaro De Bonfili were assisting the shipyard and had the authority to negotiate on its behalf.

The telephone interrupted her thoughts. The receptionist informed her that Wolfgang Meyer was on the phone; his Italian was not clear, but she gathered he needed to speak with his lawyer urgently.

"Madam Avvocato Modiano, I need to talk to you urgently. The police want to talk to me. I do not know why."

Rachele realised how nervous Wolfgang Meyer was. He was speaking formally.

"When do you need to talk to them?"

"They left a message for me at the hotel that they will come and talk to me this afternoon on behalf of the police in Monfalcone."

"What happened in Monfalcone?"

"Nothing special. As I told you, I had a meeting with Fonda Trasporti. I wanted to see them before deciding on the contract."

Rachele asked her client to wait a couple of minutes, opened a drawer, and looked for his folder. She took out the notepad to take notes. She then picked up the phone again.

"Sorry for the interruption. I will send you Dario Zago. He is part of my team. He can listen in and provide legal advice if necessary. I also suggest that you ask Carlo Kovach to assist you in communicating with the police. You will feel much more relaxed if you have organised an interpreter rather than using one provided by the police. You will know the interpreter is on your side. At what time did they say they will be there?"

Wolfgang Meyer did not sound relaxed.

"They told Carlo Kovach they will be here by 3 pm."

Rachele hoped she sounded reassuring.

"Dario will be there by half-past two. I trust him; he just qualified as a lawyer but has been working for us for three years and has a strong sense of evidence. He will help ensure that there are no misunderstandings that may inconvenience you. In the meantime, I will try to determine why the police want to speak with you. Do you have time to come and see me tomorrow morning?"

Rachele could not see that her client was beginning to relax.

"If they don't arrest me today."

Wolfgang Meyer tried to be facetious. Rachele wondered why he thought he might be arrested, but planned to discuss it with him the following morning after she had spoken to

Dario. They agreed to meet at 11 am and then ended the conversation.

She asked Dario to come to her office and called her friendly judge, Antonio Penzo. The judge replied fairly quickly.

"Avvocato Modiano, how did you know I wanted to call you?"

Rachele smiled; it was the standard opening line for a judge who, nine years earlier, had been wary of the 'daughter of an aristocratic family' who wanted to practise law to prove a point. His views on her professional capabilities had changed dramatically since then.

"I didn't. I'm not even sure you can help me; this is a 'just in case' phone conversation."

Rachele could not see the judge smiling, but she knew him well enough to know that he was.

"Is it one of your hypothetical questions?"

"It is very real. I am trying to find out if you have any information that may be relevant. Do you remember when you came to me with a contract in German that the police had found on top of the desk in a ransacked room with my business card pinned to it?"

Antonio Penzo stopped smiling. Rachele could not see it, but he adjusted his posture, sitting straighter in his chair.

"I do, and this time I wasn't joking when I asked you how you knew I was about to call you. Is Wolfgang Meyer your client?"

Dario had appeared at the door, and Rachele gestured to come in and sit in a chair on the other side of her desk. Rachele replied to the judge's question in a very circumspect tone, almost as if she were a witness in court.

"He is. We have assisted him with a contractual issue, but we are scheduled to meet tomorrow to discuss further matters. Something that led me to call you. The only thing I know is that the police will see him this afternoon, and he will talk to me in the morning. I was hoping you could give me an idea why the police want to talk to him."

"Probably for the same reason I wanted to talk to you. Enrico Fonda was found dead in his office yesterday. The police found Wolfgang Meyer's name in his diary. They just want to talk to him."

Rachele wrote 'Enrico Fonda dead' on her notepad and passed it to Dario Zago.

"So, how can I help you? You know I cannot betray my client's confidentiality or do any action that would damage him."

"But you also have an obligation to report a crime you know has been committed."

Rachele tried to maintain a neutral tone of voice, but she felt the conversation was about to take an unpleasant turn.

"You said they found Enrico Fonda dead in his office. I suspect it wasn't a heart attack. Otherwise, you would not have been involved. At this stage, I only know that the police will see my client this afternoon. Dario Zago will be with him. He will talk to me tomorrow morning, and then you and I can have our conversation."

"So, can I call you tomorrow afternoon?"

Rachele tried her best to sound matter-of-fact.

"You know you can call me anytime. You also know that tomorrow afternoon I'll share what I think I must share, or anything that might help clear my client's name."

Antonio Penzo avoided sounding patronising.

"I wouldn't expect anything else. I'll talk to you tomorrow."

After Rachele hung up, she turned to Dario.

"Go to Pensione Vivaldi. We need to establish Wolfgang Meyer's movement and determine if there are witnesses who can validate the time he arrived after his business trip. This could be quick or extremely complicated. The police are scheduled to arrive at 3 pm to speak with him. I told him you'll be there by 2.30."

Rachele noticed Gabriele was silent on their way home. The mist created a slightly out-of-focus atmosphere that made the usual buildings almost look magical. He had a tight grip on Rachele's arm, nearly using his wife as a crutch. Silence was never heavy between them, and Rachele was enjoying the sense of private intimacy in a public environment. It was the perfect way to relax, the way to decompress from work and just concentrate on walking home with her husband. She tried to force herself not to think of her brother, Wolfgang Meyer, and the deceased Enrico Fonda. Gabriele had turned right after the Rialto Bridge, and walking by the Rialto market was a way to extend their walk home. Once they crossed Rio de le Becarie, she was ready to talk.

"How was your day?"

Gabriele reacted to his wife's voice almost as if somebody had woken him up from a deep sleep.

"I had a long meeting with the team that is running the project of the road bridge. We have discussed how they are going to disrupt navigation in the canals around the area that will be demolished to make way for the area where the road will end. We reviewed the list of buildings to be demolished and the scaffolding required to be built on the canal side of each building. It was a very intense day. It was great to decompress. How was your day?"

Rachele sensed her husband was now relaxing; his grip on her arm had loosened, and he even had a hint of a smile.

"Oh, the usual, contracts, family potential legal issues, and, by mid-morning, somebody being murdered."

Gabriele smiled at the light-hearted way his wife described her day.

"Is your family's potential legal issue connected with the murder in any way?"

Rachele, a Jewish lawyer, found that answering a question with another question came naturally to her.

"What makes you say that?"

"Just the way you listed the highlights of your day."

Rachele stopped walking.

"I sincerely hope not! Although Daniele told me that he paid a visit to Fonda Trasporti to see what he could do to help his close friend, Franz Sedlak. Since I talked to him early this morning, I did not know I should have asked more questions, so I'll talk to him again tomorrow."

Gabriele sensed his wife would prefer not to talk about work, so once they crossed Rio de San Cassan, he changed the subject after walking in silence for a while.

"When are your parents and my parents expected for dinner?"

"They should already be there, playing with their granddaughters. It is a working day dinner, mostly leftovers from yesterday's birthday party. Mum and Dad are going back to Trieste tomorrow. By the way, don't delude yourself, they are there to be grandparents. We could go out tonight, and they would not notice."

Chapter Eight

February 1930

25 February 1930

It was Rachele's turn to get Emma and Anna ready for breakfast. She fed Diana, who had become very punctual in letting her mother know she was hungry. When it was time to wake up Emma and Anna, she had the usual battle to get them washed and dressed. She was slightly less accommodating than her husband; she did not take any nonsense, and her daughters knew better than to complain or try to delay getting up. When they entered the kitchen, Anita had already sorted out the girls' breakfast, and Gabriele was making coffee for the adults. She sat Emma and Anna at the breakfast table, put Diana in her high chair so she could be with everybody else. Gabriele poured her coffee, and she drank her first cup. Her brain was ready to function.

"Anita, did you find out from Fiamma what we are supposed to contribute to Saturday lunch?"

Anita had just finished checking what she needed to buy after dropping Emma and Anna off at nursery school. She walked out of the pantry with her list.

"You need to bake the usual, only more of them. On Friday morning, I go there to help Fiamma prepare the meat and the vegetables. Myriam will collect Emma and Anna from school, and you and Gabriele will have lunch with us."

Gabriele lifted his head from the paper.

"When did you decide? I spoke to my father last night, and he did not mention any of that, including us going to lunch on Friday."

Rachele and Anita looked at each other, smiling. Anita sat down for her cup of coffee.

"Probably because organising the food for the big lunch with Myriam's future in-laws did not involve him."

Rachele added, smiling.

"That's because you and your father don't cook, so Fiamma decided not to involve you. I am sure she'll have other tasks for you if you feel left out."

Then she went back to paying attention to her daughters.

Dario was reviewing his notes from the previous day's visit to Pensione Vivaldi.

"Carlo Kovach will make a great witness, you should speak with him about the researcher role, unless you have already decided whom to hire. He has a keen sense of which information is relevant. He told me how to contact Matteo Masiero, the Taxi driver who collected Wolfgang Meyer from the station and took him to the hotel."

Dario knew Rachele had been listening and looking for Wolfgang Meyer's folder. She smiled when she found it.

"So, we can trace his movement back to Venice if we have to. How was the conversation with the police?"

"They asked him some basic questions, like when he met Enrico Fonda, when he left Fonda Trasporti, and which train he took to come back to Venice. They will speak with the police in Monfalcone, and if necessary, they will speak with him again. Do you know why?"

"Not really, but yesterday I had an interesting telephone conversation with Judge Antonio Penzo, so I wanted to be prepared. I am waiting for Wolfgang Meyer to tell me why the police are interested in him, so I can understand if it is connected with yesterday's call with Judge Penzo."

Dario closed his notepad.

"Which you are keeping private."

Rachele smiled and tried not to sound patronising.

"Until I am sure it applies to whatever Wolfgang Meyer will tell me in about an hour. Now, can we talk about why you think Carlo Kovach could be an excellent replacement for your investigative skills after you start working here as a trainee lawyer?"

An hour later, a secretary came to tell her that Wolfgang Meyer had arrived and was waiting for her in one of the meeting rooms. Rachele picked up her folder and a notepad. On her way to the meeting room, she asked Franco Venier's secretary to find a slot in his diary for a meeting in the afternoon. When she entered the meeting room, she found him pacing back and forth across the room.

"Good morning, Mr Meyer. Please sit down and start from the beginning."

The manners that had been drummed into Rachele's head throughout her childhood prevented her from sitting until her guest had sat down, but Wolfgang Meyer was too tense to think of manners. Instead of insisting, Rachele sat and pointed to the chair on the other side of the table. Her client looked as if he had been brought down to earth and sat down.

"After I visited clients in Triest and Görz[i], I had some time left. I telephoned Fonda Trasporti, asking to meet the director, Enrico Fonda, on my way back to Venice. I arrived at Monfalcone station, left my luggage there, and went to inspect Fonda Trasporti. The meeting lasted an hour, then I left, collected my luggage, and took the train to Venice. Yesterday I found out that somebody killed Enrico Fonda, and his meeting with me was the latest entry in his diary before the time of death."

"Were you cautioned in any way?"

"No, but after your researcher left, they called and told me they want to see me again today at 3 pm, at the police headquarters."

"We haven't billed you yet, so I am still your lawyer. I'll come as your interpreter. "

They agreed Rachele would go to Pensione Vivaldi right after her lunch break, and they would go to the police together. She also expected to find Judge Penzo there, but she did not tell her client. Wolfgang Meyer left the meeting more relaxed than when he arrived.

On her way to her office, Rachele wanted to check the 'kosher cupboard' in the kitchen, where the firm was keeping refreshments acceptable to her and Alvise. She was the leading provider of baked goods for the cupboard, and since she had two heavy baking sessions for the family lunch on Saturday, she might just add something for the office as well. She found Alvise Cantoni looking for something to eat. They hadn't crossed paths in a while, so she stopped to chat. Alvise found the biscuit tin he was looking for. He couldn't hide his disappointment when he noticed it was empty. He put it back and turned around to face his friend and colleague.

 "On my way here, I saw the tall, blond, middle-aged man again, completely dressed in white. In broad daylight, he doesn't look like a ghost, just an eccentric man."

Rachele smiled.

"I have never seen him, but he must be a striking figure. I had reports of his sighting by many people, and they were all impressed. I understand he is a German aristocrat, Graf von Falkenberg, a regular guest of Pensione Vivaldi."

Back in her office, she summoned Dario Zago to discuss her meeting with Wolfgang Meyer and what they needed to establish, assuming the police wanted to talk to him about the death of Enrico Fonda. Once she had finished telling Dario about her meeting, she went into mentor mode.

"So, what do you think we should establish?"

Dario looked at his notes.

"Do we know the estimated time of death? We need to speak with Matteo Masiero, the taxi driver, to confirm Mr Meyer's time of arrival in Venice. We may also have to establish that he could not have had the time to kill Enrico Fonda, go to the station, or be driven to a station past Monfalcone to arrive at Venice at the time he did."

"That's more or less it. We do not know Enrico Fonda's time of death yet, but we can establish if, by any chance, the taxi driver saw Wolfgang Meyer get off the train. Talk to Carlo Kovach. You can come to the police station later and give me a note. I'll let them know you will join us..."

Dario noticed her mischievous smile before she added,

"...to be at the meeting for training purposes. You will soon be a newly qualified lawyer, after all."

Chapter Nine

February 1930

26 February 1930

Dario Zago had just got off the waterbus. The wind had made the open water of the lagoon very choppy, nothing compared to the open sea on the other side of the Lido, but still enough to make standing outside difficult. His umbrella had only symbolic value; the wind made any protection from the rain nearly impossible. Entering the café near the office was a blessed relief. He had agreed to meet with Carlo Kovach before they met with Rachele. Dario wanted to check whether Carlo would be interested in being the new researcher at the Venier-Zanin law firm. In a month, he would start working as a trainee lawyer, and the firm would have to hire a new researcher. He liked Carlo, and he thought that his experience of working as a junior concierge was very relevant to a job that often required looking inconspicuous to gather information. Dario had stopped right after the entrance; he was enjoying the warm, wind-free atmosphere when he noticed Carlo waving at him from a table in the far corner of the café, away from the crowd drinking their coffee standing at the bar. Dario waved back, caught the attention of the barman, made his order, and pointed to the table where Carlo was sitting. Once a waiter had delivered his coffee with a glass of water and a pastry, he figured out he could move from the small talk to the reason he had asked Carlo to meet him outside the office.

"In three weeks, I will be a qualified lawyer, and the Venier-Zanin law firm has offered me a job as a trainee, which means they need a researcher. Would you be interested in the position? If you are, we can discuss it with Avvocato Modiano at the end of our meeting."

Carlo Kovach finished his espresso and drank the water. He needed to buy time.

"Why did you think of me?"

Dario did not hesitate.

"You are a keen observer, and as an assistant concierge, you are used to listening, remembering the preferences of regular clients, and I noticed you keep a lot of details and have some sense of what is relevant in a conversation."

"And you think these are qualities for a researcher? Where can I go from that role? At the moment, I have no intention of studying law."

Dario was ready for that question; he had discussed it with Franco Venier, one of the two partners of the law firm.

"When you are bored with being a researcher, or when you are tired of walking around Venice, you can move to client management."

Carlo Kovach smiled and said that if he had a job offer, he

would be interested. The two young men stood up and left the café to go to the law firm.

Rachele had woken up early to bake for the big family lunch on Saturday. Luckily, her morning started well. She and Gabriele had met Alvise in a café on the other side of the Rialto Bridge to discuss Alvise's decision to move to his father's law firm. She arrived at her desk with a big smile on her face, half an hour before her meeting with Carlo Kovach and Dario. The smile faded when she thought of Wolfgang Meyer being questioned by the police the previous afternoon. Everything hung on finding two witnesses who could testify he was on that specific train back to Venice. Even if he had an accomplice with a car willing to drive him to another station, something the police had to prove, it is unlikely that he could have killed Enrico Fonda and arrive in Venice when he said he did. She reviewed the notes she had written after the meeting with the police, added a couple of questions, and then put everything back into the Wolfgang Meyer folder. Something bothered her. She couldn't figure out what, but she knew her subconscious mind would work on it while she was concentrating on something else.

She suddenly thought about it on her way to the meeting room. When she entered the room, she apologised to Dario and Carlo. She sat down, took out the notepad from the folder, and wrote, 'Connections between the ransacked hotel room and the death of Enrico Fonda'. She apologised again and greeted Carlo Kovach properly. Dario let their guest share with Rachele what he had established while they were at the police station.

"Wolfgang Meyer uses the same taxi driver, Matteo Masiero. They have a sort of arrangement. Pensione Vivaldi also frequently uses him. I have his contact details here."

He took out his diary from his jacket pocket, looked for a page, and then passed it to Rachele, who copied the taxi driver's contact details into her notepad. He waited for her to finish writing before continuing.

"I remember it very well because two clients asked me to organise a taxi to the Lido, and I contacted Matteo Masiero, who told me he had to go to the station to meet Wolfgang Meyer. Yesterday afternoon, after speaking with Mr Zago, I tried to recall who else was at the reception when Wolfgang Meyer arrived. I checked the names on the list with my boss."

He took out a piece of paper folded in two from another pocket and passed it to Rachele. She was impressed that he had separated staff, guests, and known casual visitors. Next to the guests, there was the date they were scheduled to leave Pensione Vivaldi.

Rachele looked at Carlo Kovach.

"This is an impressive and accurate list. We now require two affidavits: one from Matteo Masiero, confirming that he saw Wolfgang Meyer getting off the train, and another from a person on this list, confirming the arrival at Pensione Vivaldi. Then I can organise the rest to ensure that our client is not charged with anything."

She then turned to Dario.

"By the way, Dario, I think your gut feeling is right. Why don't you figure out with Franco Venier's secretary when they can discuss him replacing you, provided Mr Kovach likes the idea? In the meantime, please obtain those two affidavits; the signatures also require a witness to sign. Just remember, neither of you can witness them.”

Rachele enjoyed walking around Venice on her own. Work, her husband, three daughters, a housekeeper, and the extended Mendes clan conspired to make it unusual for her to enjoy her own company. Myriam had suggested a small restaurant past the Arsenale, a place run by the parents of a friend who had a sibling with a small holding on the Island of Sant'Erasmo, the island in the Venetian lagoon that had provided fresh vegetables to Venice for centuries. The early morning wind and rain had subsided; the sun was shining, making it the perfect day as far as Rachele was concerned. She followed Myriam's directions and turned left before crossing the bridge over Rio dell'Arsenale. She saw her sister-in-law waiting for her outside the restaurant. They greeted each other, walked inside, and were shown to a table. Once the waiter had taken their orders, Myriam came to the point.

“I need your advice, and I have a favour to ask. My future mother-in-law has a first cousin from Graz. Her Italian is very poor. Do you mind if we sit her at your table?”

The waiter came with the mixed vegetable salad, put the plates in front of them, and left to fetch oil and vinegar.

“Please do, I'll talk to her. I assume that is the favour. What is the advice?”

Myriam started dressing her salad. Rachele couldn't understand the need for a delaying tactic, but waited for her sister-in-law to talk whenever she had found the right words. After a few minutes of contemplating the vegetables on her plates, Myriam lifted her head.

"How did you bring up with Gabriele that you wanted to keep working? I haven't discussed it with Michele yet. I do not know how to bring it up."

Rachele thought of the conversation she had with Gabriele the day he proposed. She couldn't help but smile at the thought of how lucky she felt then and how lucky she still felt.

"I brought up the subject the day Gabriele proposed. We had gone out for a walk after he proposed, and were about to enter Caffe degli Specchi, the historic café in Piazza dell'Unita d'Italia in Trieste. I did not expect Gabriele's reaction."

"Which was?"

"He had no hesitation, and simply said that he would support me whatever I decided to do."

Myriam smiled.

"My brother loved you so much, he would have agreed to anything."

Rachele stopped smiling.

"Your brother has supported me in every decision I've made in the past ten years. He meant it. Why did you wait until three weeks before the wedding to bring it up?"

A pause to allow the waiter to take away their plates and bring them the grilled fish they had ordered. Again, Myriam focused on unwrapping the tin foil that was used to cook the fish with the vegetables. A few minutes later, she lifted her head.

"He always said he loved what you and Gabriele had. He felt you always acted as one. I did not think that conversation was necessary."

"Why do you think it has become necessary? Why now?"

Myriam looked around and lowered her voice.

"My mother-in-law made a comment about the day I give my notice."

Rachele could not understand the caution, but she went along with a lower voice.

"Why? You have only just started working for a bank. Before your graduation, you were helping your mother in the family business. Anyway, I think you should make clear to Michele that you have no intention of resigning."

Myriam smiled and went back to a normal tone of voice.

"So, can you help me find another Anita?"

Rachele raised her hands and shrugged her shoulders.

"I'll try, but I suspect she is one of a kind. Gabriele and I won the lottery when she appeared in our lives."

They finished their meal. They both had to go back to work. Rachele told Myriam she was walking back to Rialto. She had some things to figure out before a meeting later in the afternoon. They walked together to the vaporetto stop, then Rachele hugged Myriam, told her to speak to her fiancé, waved at her sister-in-law as the vaporetto was leaving, and then started walking back to her office.

Rachele had spent most of the afternoon with her boss and a new lawyer, discussing their workload and the transition of Dario Zago from researcher to trainee lawyer. Rachele had things to discuss with Dario, so she volunteered to inform him of the practicalities associated with his new role. When Dario came into her office to discuss the Mayer case, she told him he would start as a trainee lawyer in April. They wanted time to hire a new researcher and for him to transfer all the cases he was involved in to the new guy. They also expected that, for the first couple of months, he would train his replacement and conduct any necessary research work. His pay as a trainee lawyer would start in April. Then it was Dario's turn to update her.

"On my way home, I dropped by Pensione Vivaldi to collect the affidavits of the Taxi Driver who picked up Wolfgang Meyer from the station and of another hotel guest who saw him arrive at the hotel. Carlo Kovach has sorted them out. Carlo told me that his boss had witnessed both signatures."

Rachele stopped taking notes.

"Do we know who the hotel guest is? Do you work well with Carlo Kovach?"

Dario looked at his notepad.

"The other guest is Graf von Falkenberg, and his affidavit is in German. I know you can translate it, but we may need the court to validate the translation. Working with Carlo is a pleasure. I think his job has trained him to retain a lot of information and be observant and discreet. I am not sure what his ultimate ambition is, but I think he will work as my replacement."

Rachele checked the list of names Carlo Kovach had given her the previous day.

"Graf von Falkenberg is not on this list."

"He insisted he saw the taxi arrive at Pensione Vivaldi and Wolfgang Meyer get off. He was in the café in the garden. Carlo thought he would have noticed him in the garden, but he insisted he was there."

Rachele was about to say something when the phone on her desk rang. The switchboard informed her that Matteo Masiero needed to speak with her urgently. Rachele repeated the caller's name loudly, and Dario told her he was the taxi driver who signed one of the two affidavits. She took the call.

"Good morning Mr Masiero, I am Avvocato Modiano[i]."

"Thank you for taking my call, Avvocato. Carlo Kovach gave me your phone number; I need to talk to you urgently."

"Can you give me an idea of what it's about?"

"It is in connection with Wolfgang Meyer. Perhaps it's nothing, perhaps it's important, perhaps I'm in trouble, perhaps not. Carlo thinks I shouldn't discuss it where I can be overheard."

The last statement concerned Rachele. She noticed Dario standing up and gestured for him to wait.

"Give me a moment. I need to check my diary. If we get cut off, or if you have to go, I shall leave a message with reception."

Rachele put the handset on the desk and picked up her diary, which was already opened to the right page. She picked up the handset again.

"Can you be here in an hour? Otherwise, tomorrow at 11."

"Carlo Kovach explained to me where you are. I think I can be there tomorrow at 11. A client booked me later this afternoon, and I don't know where I have to take him."

Rachele wrote the name and time in a notepad, adding, 'Are you free?' and then handed it to Dario. Once he nodded, she replied.

"That will be fine. I am looking forward to meeting you tomorrow."

She hung up, put a note in her diary, and then looked at Dario.

"He said something that worried me. It could be nothing, or it could be very important for Wolfgang Meyer, or we may have a new client. Do you have any idea why he wants to talk to us?"

"None whatsoever. I need to go. I have a meeting with Franco Venier. We'll find out tomorrow."

Rachele closed her diary.

"I guess we will."

Dario left the room. Half an hour later, a secretary came to say that Carlo Kovach had arrived with an envelope, insisting that he must deliver it in person. Rachele told her she could guess what it was and to let him come to her office. A few minutes later, Carlo Kovach appeared carrying an envelope with the two affidavits. Rachele welcomed him and told him to sit down. She opened the envelope and started reading the affidavits.

"Thank you for your work. I'll keep yours in reserve. If I were the prosecutor, I would argue that you work for the hotel or that you are about to start working for us. The other two are great. Who wrote the one in German?"

Carlo straightened up

"I did."

"Congratulations, you speak German very well. What can you tell me about Matteo Masiero?"

Carlo paused for a moment. Rachele hoped he was just organising his thoughts.

"He is one of the taxi drivers the hotel calls when we need one. He occasionally runs errands, such as picking up luggage that clients send in advance. Wolfgang Meyer uses him regularly. He only uses Matteo Masiero."

Rachele did not know whether to take notes.

"He asked to see me urgently. Any idea what he wants to talk about?"

Carlo shrugged his shoulders.

"He asked me if I knew a lawyer I trust. He needed legal advice urgently. I gave him the phone number of this law firm. That is all I know."

Dario Zago appeared at the door.

"Rachele, your husband has arrived. He and Alvise Cantoni are waiting for you at the reception. They told me to remind you that this evening you are having drinks with your sister-in-law's future in-laws. Carlo, you need to come to me to talk to Avvocato Venier."

Chapter Ten

February 1930

27 February 1930

It was a sunny winter day with all the promise of spring. Gabriele felt almost euphoric as he walked to work next to his wife. He kept pointing out signs of spring whenever a branch was leaning out of a wall or some daring boatman was facing the day without a coat. Rachele was not very talkative. He had figured out that something was bothering her, but not bothering her enough to wake up early and bake. When they crossed the second bridge, Gabriele decided to find out.

"You haven't said much this morning. What's bothering you?"

Rachele looked as if she had been brought down to earth and landed with a thud.

"I have a challenging meeting today, I am going through three affidavits to make sure a judge can allow a client to travel, also I have an intriguing meeting with one of those who wrote an affidavit, and I wonder why he needs to talk to a lawyer urgently. When he called me yesterday afternoon, he kept saying he was not comfortable discussing it over the phone."

Gabriele could not comment on what his wife had just said. He knew she was intentionally vague not to disclose any confidential matter. They were walking arm in arm, so he tightened his grip on her arm, hoping she would take it as the sign of support he intended to give her. Rachele stopped, forcing him to stop, looked at him, smiled, and then started walking again, changing the subject.

"Do you remember Anita will collect Emma and Anna from nursery school and take them to your parents? She has agreed to help Fiamma prepare tomorrow night's big meal, so we are having lunch at your parents'. By the way, Arrigo Mondani will be there as well. Sofia has to take her mother to an important doctor's appointment, and she is not sure she will be back before lunch."

Gabriele realised Rachele did not want to talk about work any further.

"Do we know what's wrong with Sofia's mother?"

"Not really, but I'm sure we'll find out by Saturday afternoon. I am sure Paolo, Sofia, and Arrigo will join us on Shabbat."

They had reached the top of Rialto's Bridge; Rachele briefly stopped for her 'Canaletto moment'. When they started walking again, they noticed Alvise Cantoni waving at them from the bottom of the steps. Gabriele kissed his wife on the cheek and started walking towards his office. Rachele and Alvise started climbing the two flights of stairs to their office.

Rachele was discussing the team she had to coordinate from the following April with Franco Venier when a secretary came to tell them that Antonio Penzo had arrived and was waiting for them. They both stood up and continued the conversation on their way to the meeting room. They stopped before entering and agreed to continue it the following morning. Rachele greeted Antonio Penzo, then she excused herself, she had to go to her office to collect the affidavit and her notepad, leaving the judge with her boss, a close friend of the judge.

Less than ten minutes later, she was back. She noticed somebody had taken care of refreshments. Franco Venier left them to discuss business after making sure the judge would stop by his office before leaving so they could arrange the details for a forthcoming social engagement. Once her boss had left the room, they sat down, and Rachele took out the affidavits in order. Before she started discussing them, her visitor had a question.

"As you know, I trust your guts. When the police in Monfalcone contacted us, I thought the name of the company where they found the body rang a bell. Do you think the murder of Enrico Fonda is somehow connected with the unusual clause in the contracts found in Wolfgang Mayer's ransacked room?"

Rachele opened the folder with the affidavits. She looked at the judge with a face showing all her doubts.

"I have been thinking about that connection for a few days. I think there must be one, but I can't think of a possible one."

Rachele recovered and brought the conversation back where she wanted it. She took one of the affidavits and pushed it towards the magistrate.

"Wolfgang Meyer stated that he paid a visit to Fonda Trasporti to find out about the clause in the contract. He had arranged the appointment with Enrico Fonda, and they managed to understand each other in a mixture of Italian and German. The affidavit signed by Mr Meyer is in German but I translated it into Italian, and I added a statement to that effect, then signed it. I am prepared to swear that the translated text matches the original in German."

Antonio Penzo read the Italian translation, showing no reaction. When he reached the end, he simply countersigned Rachele's statement about the translation. She noticed it and pushed two other statements.

"There is another affidavit of the taxi driver, Matteo Masiero, who picked up Wolfgang Meyer at the station when he arrived back in Venice. The third is also in German, with a translation I verified. The signatory is Graf Wilhelm von Falkenberg, a guest staying at Pensione Vivaldi, who saw Wolfgang Meyer arrive at the hotel when he was sitting at the café in the garden."

Antonio Penzo took the other two affidavits, but he did not read them.

"Basically, two people confirm the time Wolfgang Meyer arrived back in Venice, which matches his statement, so by the time Enrico Fonda died, the train had already reached Mestre."

Rachele had prepared another document for the magistrate.

"So you can sign the statement that Wolfgang Meyer is authorised to leave Venice. Just in case he needs one."

"Yes, of course. I still want to talk to him; he could provide interesting information."

"He leaves for Milan Monday afternoon. He is due to come here to pick up this letter and settle his bill on Monday morning. You can arrange to talk to him then, Dario will be with him. He will be a qualified lawyer in two weeks."

Rachele passed the folder to Antonio Penzo so he could place the affidavits back inside before putting them in his briefcase. He looked at her smiling.

"And he is happy to work here. I still think he would make a great prosecutor."

"He will be a great lawyer, wherever he works, but he is happy to work here. He will be part of my team."

"You can't blame a man for trying."

Rachele had had some time with Dario before the scheduled meeting with Matteo Masiero. They were talking in the meeting room when the receptionist came to inform them that their visitor had arrived and led them to the meeting room where he was waiting. She took orders for refreshments and left. Rachele introduced herself and Dario Zago. She noticed her visitor had no apparent reaction to meeting a woman who practiced law, and she smiled inwardly. The receptionist entered with coffee, water, and a plate with biscuits and immediately left. Matteo Masiero's posture changed; he was getting nervous.

"Carlo Kovach of Pensione Vivaldi suggested I talk to you. I am not even sure I need a lawyer, but he thought I'd better talk to one."

Rachele's and Dario's silence pushed him to continue.

"Wolfgang Meyer is one of my regular clients. I have four who come to Pensione Vivaldi regularly. They let the hotel know when I have to pick them up at the station. I also take Mr Meyer to the station when he leaves Venice. Usually, he asks me to deliver one of his pieces of luggage to San Giuliano. At the other end of the railway bridge, he told me that a shipping company he knows will take it back to Zurich. The luggage is locked, and I don't know what is inside."

Dario Zago noticed Rachele was taking notes. He was listening and wondering why Matteo Masiero felt the need to consult a lawyer.

"So far, nothing is even remotely illegal or could risk damages. To whom do you deliver the bag, or suitcase?"

Their visitor looked at Dario.

"Let me finish. I leave the luggage on the quay, blow the horn twice, wait for a car door to open, then I go. I seldom see the person who comes to collect the bag."

Rachele stopped taking notes and looked at Dario. Things were getting interesting.

"Well, last time, when I took Wolfgang Meyer to the station, he left a canvas bag on the boat. When I picked it up to deliver it, I noticed a hole. From the hole, I could see something yellow and shiny. Judged from the weight, I think I was delivering gold. Am I in trouble?"

Rachele and Dario looked at each other. They now could understand why he needed a lawyer. Rachele put down the pen and notepad.

"I think you were right. I don't think you're necessarily in trouble, but you need to prove your good faith. You need legal help to avoid being accused of being an accomplice in gold smuggling, if that is indeed the case. A lawyer can ensure that you are protected and may advise you. Unfortunately, I cannot give you an immediate answer whether I can accept you as a client or I need to refer you to a colleague."

"Why?"

"Because I already represent Wolfgang Meyer, I need to discuss your case with colleagues to decide whether there is a potential conflict of interest or a joint problem. What we can do now is you can sign the paperwork to become a client, and then we will name the lawyer after my conversation with colleagues."

Rachele could see the question mark on Matteo Masiero's face, so she clarified.

"You need to sign the form so every conversation about you we have internally stays confidential. It is for your protection."

Matteo Masiero's face visibly relaxed. Rachele asked Dario to fetch the forms from reception. When he came back, he gave the form to Matteo Masiero for him to fill out. Once he had completed and signed the form, she added.

"Now we are bound by confidentiality, even for this meeting. What you say will not be discussed with anybody outside the firm. We have a meeting to discuss cases this afternoon. I'll let you know tomorrow whether I can represent you or one of my colleagues will."

Matteo Masiero stood up.

"I think I could be here tomorrow in the late morning. I could find out in person."

Rachele looked at Dario, who figured out what the look meant.

"Mr Masiero, let me take you to the secretary who manages our diaries so we can see when Avvocato Modiano is free tomorrow in the late morning."

The meeting to review major cases at the law firm went well; the overall consensus was that there was no conflict of interest, unless Wolfgang Meyer was aware that he was smuggling gold into Italy. When Gabriele arrived to walk home with her, he found his wife in an excellent mood, which was exactly what he needed. He had a lengthy meeting to discuss project details related to the road bridge to the mainland. This time, Rachele was talkative, but her husband was not reacting beyond a single complete sentence; often, his response was purely monosyllabic. Rachele knew he wanted to leave work at work, and that day it proved difficult. They were having lunch at Gabriele's parents, not on their usual walk home. Once they crossed the bridge at the end of Strada Nova, she decided it was time to intervene.

"What happened at work? Are you still thinking about it?"

Gabriele reacted as if he had just come down to earth.

"Sorry, does it show? The project for the road bridge requires an area where vehicles can arrive in Venice, park, and turn around. That implies demolishing homes, warehouses, and other commercial buildings. My mind is still trying to figure out the extent of the work and the involvement of my office."

Rachele understood he had trouble removing his mind from work issues.

"Would it help to talk about it?"

"I am not sure. I don't want to talk about it. Time to concentrate on the rest of our day and hope that the back of my mind does the work."

Rachele tightened her grip on Gabriele's arm.

"I am a firm believer in the power of the back of one's mind. Very often it leads me to the solution. Leave a notepad and a pen on your bedside table, just in case you wake up with the solution to the problem."

Gabriele changed the subject while they crossed the bridge over Rio di San Marcuola.

"Did my mother tell you what you need to contribute to next Shabbat's big lunch?"

Rachele loosened her grip. She realised Gabriele's mind was not thinking of work anymore.

"I am sure she and Anita compiled a list this morning. Meanwhile, Aunt Deborah should have collected Emma and Anna's dresses for the wedding. I hope she just collected the dresses."

Gabriele stopped looking at a shop.

"Why do you say that?"

"Because every time she and our mothers go shopping for our daughters, they do not just buy one item. Sometimes I feel sorry for the customers who enter the shop after they have gone. They will find a considerably reduced stock."

Gabriele's laughter reassured Rachele.

When they arrived at Gabriele's parents' home, two very elegant daughters were showing off their new dresses under strict supervision. Anita, Fiamma, and the Countess were making sure they would not get the dresses dirty. Immediately after Emma and Anna had kissed their parents, Countess Deborah announced.

"Great, your parents have seen how beautiful you look in those dresses. You can go with me and your grandmother to take them off and change into the clothes you were wearing before I arrived."

Anita, Rachele, and Gabriele moved to the kitchen to make sure they wouldn't be overheard. Anita told them she was surprised they had just bought the two dresses, plus something matching for Diana. Gabriele was surprised they had listened to them. They were discussing the list when the Countess entered the kitchen.

"Rachele, your parents will arrive next Thursday morning. Would you like to join us for dinner? If Anita doesn't mind watching the girls, of course."

Rachele replied quickly, before Anita could say anything.

"I think it is easier if you, Uncle Viktor, my parents, Fiamma, and Samuele all come to us. It is not a big deal, and it will be a respite for Fiamma from all the work generated by Myriam's wedding."

Fiamma appeared in the kitchen with a list.

"Rachele, this is what I thought you could contribute to next Shabbat meals."

Rachele took the note, smiled, and passed it on to Anita. They looked at each other, then Anita looked at the list and turned to Fiamma.

"I will also come and help this week as much as I can."

Lunch and time with the family had relaxed both of them. They walked in comfortable silence until they reached Strada Nova. As they were looking at a shop window, Gabriele suddenly changed the subject.

"My parents, your parents, aunt Deborah, and uncle Viktor, for a long weekend and a wedding. Our daughters and my brother's children will be so spoiled that it will take at least a couple of weeks before they settle back into their routines."

Rachele looked at him.

"You forget your siblings and my siblings. They will be co-conspirators in the plot to spoil our daughters and their cousins."

28 February 1930

Rachele was in a good mood. On the way to work, she had discussed the weekend with Gabriele. They both had a tiresome week, and they were looking forward to spending time with their daughters. When she arrived at the office, the receptionist remarked that she looked very cheerful. She had barely settled at her desk when the phone rang. She was surprised to hear Antonio Penzo's voice.

He told her about a telegram he had just received from the Zurich police requesting assistance. They were investigating a gold smuggling ring. Venice was one port they used to send gold to Brazil or Argentina. The organisation used blackmail to persuade people travelling to Venice to take a locked suitcase containing gold bars. The people involved did not know what was in the suitcase or bag they were taking to Venice.

"Do you think Wolfgang Meyer is one of those innocent couriers?"

Rachele had connected the dots the moment she heard 'gold smuggling'.

"Maybe that would explain his room being ransacked. However, I may have information about the gold smuggling ring on Monday, if my final meeting of the week goes the way I expect."

She could hear Antonio Penzo's laughter. She reacted promptly.

"Well, I thought you called about our meeting on Monday, and you surprised me with a gold smuggling ring. It is only fair that I am left with the opportunity to surprise you."

Antonio Penzo was still laughing.

"I have learnt never to be surprised by anything you say or do. How do you greet fellow Jews on Fridays? Shabbat Shalom? Is it correct?"

Rachele confirmed it was correct, then wished him a good weekend before hanging up.

She immediately wrote a note about the gold smuggling ring and included it in Wolfgang Meyer's folder. Then, she took out an empty folder, wrote 'Matteo Masiero' on the cover, prepared another note, and put that inside the folder. She was looking at her diary for the following week when Dario came to tell her that their new client had arrived. When they joined Matteo Masiero in the meeting room, she came straight to the point.

"My colleagues agree that there is no apparent conflict of interests between you and Wolfgang Meyer, but I have to tell you that, in the future, if I think that helping him would hurt you, or vice versa, I will pass you to a colleague who is not on my team because Wolfgang Meyer has been my client for longer."

Matteo Masiero had no problem with that. He countersigned the lawyer's name in his client's induction form (all copies), folded his copy, and put it in the inside pocket of his jacket. Rachele waited for him to finish before springing a surprise.

"Are you available Monday in the late morning?"

"I only have two journeys to the railway station booked. Why?"

"I have just been informed about a gold smuggling ring. Monday morning, a magistrate will come to this office to sign papers for a matter concerning Wolfgang Meyer. Would you be available to cooperate with the police?"

He said he would. Rachele asked him to tell her anything he thought applied to what, for him, was 'the case of the broken canvas bag'. He complied. During his tale, Dario and Rachele frequently exchanged glances.

Chapter Eleven

March 1930

03 March 1930

Rachele was baking. She was not tense or anxious about something at work; the list her mother-in-law had given her was too much to be sorted out in one day. She was in the middle of preparing the pistachio cream for the pistachio pie when Anita walked into the kitchen, greeted her, and started working on coffee.

"I had one already, but I wouldn't mind a second one. Anita, could you possibly wash the small coffee machine? I am sorry to ask you to do that, but I want to sort out the pistachio pies for us and for the big Shabbat."

Anita had already started washing what was in the sink, waiting for the coffee to brew. She took out cups and saucers and began preparing the table for the grown-up breakfast on one side and the children's breakfast on the other.

"At what time do we need to be there on Sunday? I have

promised Fiamma that I will organise breakfast. She will be busy helping Myriam."

"So will we, I mean her three daughters-in-law and Sarah Pesaro De Bonfili. We take the place of the sisters Myriam doesn't have."

Rachele stopped talking because they heard Diana cry. It was a bit early for her, but she was hungry. Rachele had her hands in the dough for the cake. She looked at Anita, who immediately understood what had to be done. She started warming up the water for the formula and took out the bottle with water and baby tea from the icebox, warming it up in a saucepan.

By the time Gabriele came into the kitchen holding Diana, the bottle with water and the baby tea was warm enough to give something to Diana, while the baby formula was cooling off. Gabriele looked at his wife.

"Pistachio pie is too important. Keep going. Anita and I will sort out the girls."

Gabriele and Rachele were on their way to work. They were both relieved that the hectic beginning of the day was behind them. Myriam's wedding was the obvious subject of conversation until Rachele changed it.

"Can we pause talking about your sister's wedding? I need your opinion on something. Later this morning, I meet a client who may or may not be involved in a crime, not as a victim but as an accomplice. I don't enjoy defending criminals. So far, I have always had a reason to ditch clients who did something illegal without a valid reason I could use in court."

Gabriele knew his wife had been thinking about her predicament when they were discussing the wedding.

"Do you know your client has been an accomplice to a crime? What do your guts say?"

Rachele was silent for a short while.

"My guts tell me he was not, but there is a possibility. He is a witness to murder, and this morning, Antonio Penzo will give him a letter that clears him to travel back home, provided he agrees to come back if his testimony is required at the trial."

"Do you see him before Antonio Penzo arrives?"

"Yes, about an hour earlier."

Gabriele stopped walking and looked at his wife.

"Then, can you ask him and decide after you hear his answer? You are an excellent judge of people; your instincts will tell you whether he is telling you the truth. After you have discussed it with him, you can make your decision."

They were close to the Rialto Bridge. Rachele smiled and thanked her husband. They walked up the bridge in silence, stopped on the top for her 'Canaletto moment', then walked to Rachele's office. Gabriele kissed her on the cheek and watched her climb the stairs to her office before leaving the building to walk to his office.

Rachele followed her husband's advice. When Wolfgang Meyer arrived, she told him about the Swiss police's telegram and the smuggling of gold bars. His face looked almost relieved when he talked.

"I am forced to help make sure that a suitcase or a bag is delivered to a shipping company here in Venice. They send it early in my name and give me the receipt. Then I collect it from the left luggage counter at the railway station and take it to Pensione Vivaldi with the rest of my luggage. When I leave, Matteo Masiero comes to take me to the station, and I leave the bag in his water taxi. I think he takes it to the Austrian Fort, but the address is on the back of the luggage tag. The bag is locked with two seals to allow them to detect whether it has been tampered with. I do not know what is inside."

Rachele started writing notes.

"You are still my client, and our conversation is confidential. May I ask you why you do that?"

"Would it be enough if I said that my wife and I are being blackmailed without giving you any details?"

Rachele stopped writing

"It is fine for now, but you may have to tell me or the police later. When the magistrate, Antonio Penzo, arrives in half an hour, let me talk. Meanwhile, I need to tell accounts it is not a final bill. They have to prepare a different invoice."

Rachele wondered why Wolfgang Meyer looked so relieved. She forgot to check if he agreed to discuss it with a magistrate, but since he did not react to her recommendation to let her talk about it, she assumed he had no problem. She made a mental note to ask him when she returned to the meeting room.

Half an hour later, Antonio Penzo joined them. The meeting started with Rachele writing a German translation for Wolfgang Meyer, who read the German first and then began reading the Italian, checking the odd words with Rachele. In the end, he just had one question before he signed. He turned to Rachele, speaking German.

"Could you possibly ask Mr Judge Penzo[i] if the last paragraph means he could get the police in Zurich to take me to the station if I am not in Venice three days before the date in the letter I am supposed to receive from him?"

Rachele asked the question. The magistrate replied in Italian.

"Yes, it does. The three days would allow you to reach Venice in time if we have to use the Zurich police to convince you to come to Venice. I guess it was one day to get you organised, one day to reach Milan, and the third to arrive in Venice."

Wolfgang Meyer nodded to Rachele to show he understood and signed the two copies of the letter next to Antonio Penzo's signature. The magistrate put away his copy in a folder and was about to put it in his briefcase when Rachele looked at her client, who nodded.

"There is another thing to discuss, something I discovered only Friday morning."

She then shared with Antonio Penzo what Wolfgang Meyer had told her when they met, adding that it matched Matteo Masiero's story, and by the way, she was representing him as well.

The magistrate thanked her for the comment, took out the affidavit they had just signed, read it, and smiled. The wording was vague enough that it could apply to however many trials or investigations required Mr Meyer's testimony.

"The letter is generic enough, but I have to inform the police in Zurich about what I have just found out."

There was no need to translate, for Wolfgang Meyer had understood and nodded his head in agreement.

Rachele excused herself and followed her client outside. A short while later, she was back in the meeting room talking to the junior judge.

"Would you like to discuss the new development later today? This afternoon I am free after 4."

Antonio Penzo nodded

"Great, I'll come back around 4.30 and talk Franco into buying me a drink once we have finished."

After seeing the judge out, she went in search of Dario Zago. She asked him to go to the left luggage office at the station and determine the exact process of retrieving luggage that had been shipped before the owner's arrival.

Rachele was ready to leave for lunch. Gabriele had arrived about five minutes earlier. They were talking to Alvise Cantoni in the hall when the receptionist informed Rachele that her brother, Daniele, needed to speak to her urgently. Rachele replied she would call him back within five minutes, excused herself, and returned to her office. She sat down and did not remove her coat. Once her brother answered the call, she came straight to the point.

"I am about to leave for lunch. What happened?"

"The police in Monfalcone sent me an official summons to talk to me in connection with the death of Enrico Fonda."

Rachele sat down and removed her hat.

"Is it a problem if I call you from home after lunch?"

"Provided you let Emma and Anna say hello to their uncle Daniele."

As they were crossing the Rialto Bridge, Gabriele realised his wife had just skipped her 'Canaletto moment', a sign that something was bothering her.

"You look worried. Can you talk about it?"

Rachele looked as if she had just returned from miles away.

"After lunch, I need to call my brother Daniele. Apparently, he paid a visit to somebody shortly before he was found dead, and now the police have summoned him. He wants to say hello to Emma and Anna, and then you must remove them from the study so I can talk to him."

Gabriele realised there was more to the story but appreciated that his wife felt she was not free to share it with him or anybody outside the law firm. He changed the subject.

"I love the idea that Myriam's sisters-in-law are acting as her sisters for her wedding, although I am unsure what you should do. I have never been a bride's sister."

He noticed a smile on his wife's face. Just what he hoped he would get with his last statement. Rachele's light-hearted tone of voice confirmed it.

"Haven't you? I wonder why. Your mother explained it to me. There will be a small refreshment[ii]. We must help the bride get dressed and keep her company until it is time to walk to Scola Canton[iii]. Your baby brother, Roberto, is supposed to come and tell us when the groom has arrived with the men, and then we are right behind her when we walk to synagogue with the other women. Her mother and future mother-in-law will be behind us, ahead of all the other female guests."

That was the description of a tradition of the Mendes family. Rachele did not know where it came from, but she liked it. They got married in Trieste. Gabriele was curious whether she would have loved it.

"We did not have that because we did not get married in Venice. Would you have loved it?"

Rachele thought about it for a short time.

"To tell the truth, the first part is not very different from what happened to me with my sisters helping me get dressed and relax. My parents and I drove to synagogue in the family car with our driver; the rest of the family had organised taxis. I guess your family has a tradition adapted to the unique nature of Venice."

When they left to return to work after lunch, Rachele felt the day's chill, maybe because she was worried about her brother. She and Gabriele were walking arm-in-arm. She tightened their grip and tried her best to think of something else.

"We need to go clothes shopping. Emma and Anna are growing up."

Gabriele knew better than to ask anything about her conversation with Daniele Modiano. He followed her lead.

"They have a lot of clothes, Anna could wear some of Emma's hand-me-downs."

Rachele's grip on his arm was still tight.

"Of course, but we must also buy something new for Anna. Otherwise, we have a revolution in our midst."

Gabriele was trying to be facetious...

"Maybe we should drop a hint to the grandmothers."

...with no success. Rachele might have relaxed, but her sense of humour had barely returned.

"If you do that, they will buy two new wardrobes."

Gabriele sensed that the conversation was still bothering his wife. He knew she would tell him whenever Rachele-the-lawyer allowed Rachele-the-sister to express her feelings.

As soon as she walked through the front door of the law firm, she asked the receptionist when Franco Venier was available. She replied that he had just arrived and had no meetings scheduled for the next two hours. She turned around to check the internal switchboard and said he was not on the phone. Rachele thanked her and went to talk to her boss without stopping by her office to drop off her coat or her briefcase. The door was open, so she knocked on the doorpost. Her boss told her to enter and take a seat.

"My brother needs my professional help. I need to represent him. I am sure my time will be compensated, but I must start immediately."

She then explained to Franco Venier how her father and her uncle were trying to help the son of a recently deceased close friend save the family shipyard. Franz Sedlak, the current owner of the shipyard, was her brother Daniele's closest friend, like Alvise Cantoni and her husband. The contract her father and her uncle had asked her to look at, the one with the bizarre clause about Fonda Trasporti, was for a loan to Franz Sedlak's shipyard. Daniele wanted to find out more about

Fonda Trasporti, so he had arranged to meet Enrico Fonda the day he was found dead. He told her he was alive when he left, and Enrico Fonda's sister could confirm that. He had been summoned by the police in Monfalcone and had asked for her help.

"I have no problems with you supporting your brother. You can use any resource of this firm. Do you mind if I ask your father if we can include this in his retainer? I think it sounds better if it comes from me. Whatever his answer, my first reaction stands. This firm will support your brother."

Rachele was visibly relaxed. Franco Venier realised she had completely forgotten she was still wearing her coat. She stood up.

"Thank you. I'd better return to my office and call my brother back. I have a few questions for him before I can advise him."

"Go and take your coat off, in case you haven't noticed, the heating works. You don't need to wear your coat inside."

Chapter Twelve

March 1930

10 March 1930

Everybody slept late the day after Myriam's wedding. Gabriele and Rachele had both taken the morning off from work. Emma and Anna were unsettled, but had had a great time with their cousins and Myriam's new nephews and nieces. Diana was everybody's wake-up call. At six months, she was hungry, and the previous day's festivities did not matter. Rachele stumbled into the kitchen to sort out the formula, only to find that Anita was boiling water; her quizzical look made her friend feel she had to explain.

"I just woke up at the usual time, so I thought I'd do something useful. I had a great time yesterday. Fiamma and Myriam made me feel part of the family. Myriam introduced me as her young aunt."

Rachele had put Diana in her chair and was preparing her formula. Her youngest daughter had stopped crying and was observing what her mother was doing. She had figured out that food was on the way.

"You are part of the family, the children's Aunt Anita. Myriam introducing you as her aunt was normal; she was sixteen when you joined the family. She and Roberto took to calling you aunt fairly quickly."

Gabriele appeared in the kitchen, interrupting their conversation.

"I did not hear Diana crying or you getting up, sorry. Is there coffee or should I make it?"

Anita was busy sorting out Emma and Anna's breakfast. She didn't stop what she was doing or even turn around.

"Good morning, Gabriele, it should still be warm. Your cups and saucers are on the breakfast table. If the coffee is too cold, I'll make you a fresh one."

Rachele tried to crack a joke when the phone rang, mentioning trouble in paradise. She gave the freshly prepared bottle to Gabriele and answered the phone. After the usual greetings, Dario Zago came straight to the point.

"I hate to disturb you, but Antonio Penzo wants to talk to you in the afternoon. He wants to know if you are available at four; Matteo Masiero also wants to talk to you. He asked to leave a message with reception about the time he should come. He'll pick it up when he can this morning. What do I tell them?"

Rachele looked at her watch and realised it was already past nine. Diana did let them sleep longer, after all.

"Check my diary, but I do not remember any meeting this afternoon. Make sure that Matteo Masiero and the judge do not meet each other. I should be in by two. We are all still full from yesterday and will have a light early lunch."

"I will leave a note on your desk. I am sorry I disturbed you during your time off."

"Don't be ridiculous, you had to. Please return to the office by two, so we can talk before I meet Matteo Masiero or Judge Penzo."

Less than ten minutes after Rachele sat at his desk, Dario Zago appeared with a tray and two cups of coffee.

"Good afternoon, Dario. Thank you for the coffee. What happened? Is it very bad?"

Dario put down the tray on Rachele's desk.

"Not bad news, just a complication. When Matteo Masiero dropped by to find out the time of this afternoon's meeting, he looked distressed. The receptionist asked him if she could be of any help. He handed her an envelope, which she gave me as soon as he left."

"And?"

"The envelope had two letters with death threats."

He handed her a pair of white cotton gloves, checked that she had put them on, then gave her the envelope.

"If we take them to the police, they already have to discount my fingerprints and Matteo Masiero's; we don't want your fingerprints to complicate the search further."

Rachele took the first letter out of the envelope, read it, put it back, and did the same for the second one. She drank her coffee, then sighed.

"Do you think this is why he wanted to see me today? Did he mention where he found them?."

Dario Zago put down his cup of coffee.

"All will be revealed in twenty minutes."

Rachele opened a drawer and fished out the folder marked 'Matteo Masiero'.

"What if Masiero's threats, Meyer's break-in, and the strange clause in those contracts are connected?"

Dario had stood up to take the tray back to the kitchen. He turned around.

"What makes you think that?"

Rachele shrugged her shoulders.

"I don't know, it is a strong gut feeling. Almost like when I knew I was pregnant before I could think I was."

Dario did not hesitate.

"As the eldest of six, I remember my mother saying something similar each time she was pregnant with my youngest three siblings. I'll take it as a working assumption and see if we can prove it. See you when Mr Masiero arrives."

Rachele felt she had to clear her head after meeting Mr Masiero. He had allowed her to discuss the threats with a 'friendly magistrate' they would meet later in the afternoon. She told the receptionist that she would be back ten minutes later and walked to the top of the Rialto Bridge, hoping that a 'Canaletto moment' would clear her head. Why suddenly did she connect death threats, a break-in, and a funny clause in a contract? There must have been something she noticed that promoted that gut feeling. She stared at the Grand Canal from the top of the Rialto Bridge, but it did not help. In her mind, she had words with Canaletto for disappointing her for the first time.

When she returned to the office, the receptionist told her that Antonio Penzo had arrived early and was chatting with her boss in the kitchen. On the way to her office, Dario stopped her.

"Judge Antonio Penzo is here already, and the meeting room is available now. I thought we might start the meeting early since we have an extra item we want to discuss."

"Give me five minutes to take my coat off, pick what I need for the meeting, and then I'll join you."

The meeting lasted longer than they expected. Gabriele had already arrived and was talking to Alvise Cantoni, waiting for her to finish. She popped out of the meeting room and told him they were almost done and would be ready to leave in less than half an hour. Meanwhile, Gabriele could go to her office and telephone Anita to tell her they will be late. Then, she went back inside and tried to summarise what they knew.

"First coincidence, three people who do not know each other came to us to discuss an unusual clause in contracts associated with three different loans. The Swiss Bank insisted that a company based in Monfalcone, Fonda Trasporti, fulfilled all their shipping requirements. This is our starting point. Then the hotel room of one of our three clients, Wolfgang Meyer, was broken into, and to this day, we do not know if anything was taken. Wolfgang Meyer extends a business trip and meets with Enrico Fonda, a director of Fonda Trasporti, on the day somebody killed him."

Antonio Penzo added

"You have proven that Wolfgang Meyer could not possibly have done it because he was on a train back to Venice at the time of death."

Dario noticed Rachele masked her annoyance at being interrupted very well. She knew she had to be nice to their 'friendly judge'. She continued.

"On the same day, my brother also met Enrico Fonda, and the police want to talk to him."

Antonio Penzo was completely unaware that Rachele disliked being interrupted.

"Then Zurich police inform us they suspect that people smuggling gold out of Switzerland use Venice as the port to take gold outside Europe, and that is the only thing they know."

Dario Zago felt he had to add something just for the thrill of interrupting his boss and getting away with it.

"Then, Matteo Masiero comes to us because a bag Wolfgang Meyer gave him to be delivered to somebody in Marghera accidentally ripped, and he realised there was gold inside. The bag was locked, but the rip was large enough to see gold bars. When he delivered it, the person who took it was unhappy."

Antonio Penzo stepped in

"Do we have a description of this man?"

Rachele looked at the notes inside Matteo Masiero's folder.

"Only very generic, as in tall and broad-shouldered. He was wearing a balaclava. The day was cold and foggy, and Matteo

Masiero did not think it was a disguise. Now he has found two letters threatening to kill him in his taxi. The second one clearly relates to the first. Somebody hid them so he could find them only if he cleaned the boat, which he does every evening."

There was a pause. Dario thought she had finished, so he could add something.

"I didn't mention it when we met him earlier, but that clearly shows that somebody followed him and learnt his habits."

Antonio Penzo started putting things away.

"And that person must have used his taxi twice to hide the letters."

Rachele looked at her watch.

"Gentlemen, I think that must be all for now. We cannot solve this today, but we may think about it for a few days and meet again at a mutually convenient time later in the week, unless something unforeseen happens. Dario, have somebody call Judge Penzo's assistant to organise another meeting in two or three days, after we have had time to think about this chain of events. I need to rescue Gabriele before he falls asleep at my desk."

Gabriele had figured out that his wife had a long and intense day. The conversation for the first few minutes was mostly him talking and Rachele giving monosyllabic answers. By the time they were halfway through the Sottoportego Rialto, she was obviously beginning to relax.

"I have taken Thursday off to help Anita take the girls to synagogue to listen to the story of Esther.[i] After synagogue, we'll have lunch with your parents, and then all the cousins, Arrigo, and Franco, will have a party."

Gabriele stopped to look at a shop.

"I am sorry I can't be there. We do not have a complete plan of the works required at the Venice end of the road bridge to the mainland. So, I haven't started looking at applications for scaffolding or temporary items in or near the canals."

Rachele pulled him away from the shop.

"Come on, I'm hungry, and I feel bad if we leave Anita alone for the 'let's get ready for bed' battle."

They keep walking in silence until the bridge over Rio de le Becarie.

"Any news you can share about Daniele?"

Rachele tightened her grip on her husband's arm.

"They only want to talk to him as a potential witness. He and Enrico Fonda's sister are the last two people who saw him alive."

Gabriele did not like the image of his brother-in-law as a suspect.

"Any chance they could pin the murder on him?"

"I don't think so, but I need to talk to him more. I'll have a better idea by lunchtime tomorrow."

Chapter Thirteen

March 1930

17 March 1930

Gabriele and Anita realised Rachele was not in a great mood. As much as she loved her job, she also loved her weekends. Her brother's involvement in a murder had blurred that separation. Her father and her uncle Viktor had the same principle of keeping the weekend separate from the working week. Daniele Modiano did not.

After saying goodbye to Anita and hugging and kissing Emma, Anna, and Diana, they walked in silence for a bit. After they crossed the bridge over Rio di San Boldo, Rachele started venting her frustration.

"I believe Daniele has nothing to do with the death of Enrico Fonda, and I am prepared to do everything I can to help him. I also understand it is an emergency, but he rang me five times yesterday. I only had half a weekend. You ended up talking to Paolo and Sofia in the campo while watching Emma, Anna, and Arrigo play with the other children. I missed that because I had to reassure my brother. Bless him."

Gabriele understood his wife, but felt he had to say something to support his brother-in-law.

"I understand, but be patient. None of your family has been involved in a murder, at least not the people I know."

Rachele loosened the grip on her husband's arm and laughed.

"Well, if they have been, they kept it very well hidden from me."

Rachele spent the first half an hour at her desk trying to figure out her next steps. She worked on her circle diagram to figure out what she needed to find out. By the time Dario Zago and Carlo Kovach knocked at the doorstep of her office, she had a clear idea what they would have to do.

After greeting them and some small talk to relax, she welcomed Carlo to the firm. They both took out their notepad. She told Dario to go to Monfalcone and talk to Enrico Fonda's sister and anybody at Fonda Trasporti who remembered the visitor who saw Enrico Fonda after her brother left. Also, he was supposed to find out if the company had an agent or an office at the port of Venice. Carlo had to go to Milan to the offices of Neue Zugkredit. Dario had been there and would tell him whom he should meet. He had to find out the reason behind giving some Italian clients contracts in Italian and others in German. He should also mention that he had just started with the law firm and ask questions about the connection between the bank and Fonda Trasporti.

As she was talking, Rachele used her diagram as a reference. Dario was familiar with it, Carlo wasn't, but seemed to have figured it out pretty quickly. In the end, she moved to a more relaxed sitting position.

"Any question?"

Carlo lifted a hand to show that he needed a minute to finish writing. Dario smiled. He knew Carlo could get away with it during the first week at work, but not for long.

"Can't Dario tell me what he discovered about the connection between the two?"

Rachele picked up a pen and started playing with it.

"I'd rather not. I don't know how good an actor you are. It is a legitimate question for somebody who has started a new job and was asked to research a company."

Carlo didn't miss a beat.

"Do you think I haven't learnt to act in my previous jobs? Concierges have to smile and be kind to every client, no matter how frustrating the client is or how irritated they are."

Rachele started putting away her folders.

"You convinced me. Dario will explain things to you, then you call his contacts at the bank."

20 March 1930

It was a sunny day; spring was in the air. On their way to work, Gabriele had noticed a couple of treetops in bloom emerging from a wall alongside a canal. He would have loved a garden, but he also loved his bright home overlooking one of the few Campos with trees. They stopped at a café by the Rialto Bridge where Alvise Cantoni was waiting for them, talking to Paolo Mondani. Rachele greeted them warmly and looked at the three grown-up men who had been close friends since they were six. They had become family.

Alvise and Paolo stood up to greet them. Paolo sat down almost immediately after hugging Gabriele and Rachele. Alvise stood, ready to deliver a speech; he discussed the details behind the decision he had to make and sought his close friends' advice.

Alvise's three friends decided it was a fair arrangement, at least fair to Alvise. They started talking about getting together on a Saturday. Paolo had to go. They promised to be in touch after everybody had checked their diary and accommodated any shift Paolo might have at the hospital. The other three left as well and walked across the Rialto Bridge. Alvise and Gabriele looked at each other, rolling their eyes and smiling when Rachele stopped for her Canaletto moment at the top of the bridge.

When Rachele entered the law firm, she found Dario Zago and Carlo Kovach eagerly waiting for her. They both had something interesting to relate. Cario didn't wait to be in her office.

"Count von Falkenberg decides who gets a copy of the contract in German and who gets it in Italian. They submit all the applications to Zurich for final approval every Wednesday, and by the following Wednesday, they have the note confirming approval and specifying the language. Graf Wilhelm von Falkenberg signs the notes. I think it is the same person who is a regular guest of Pensione Vivaldi."

Rachele looked at Alvise, smiling, and turned to Carlo.

"Wait to tell me anything else when we are in the office. If that is the only thing you discovered, your trip to Milan was useful."

It was the first time Dario felt he was no longer the office junior. It felt good. He took a detour to the kitchen and joined them with a tray of water and some biscuits. Rachele lifted her head from the notes she was writing. Dario realised he had to add.

"One of the secretaries is making coffee; she will bring it as soon as it's done."

He liked Rachele's smile. They sat at the small table in her office. Rachele sorted out all her folders and the notepad with her diagrams. Dario smiled at Carlo, who was impatient to continue.

"I described the Count von Falkenberg I knew, and he agreed with the description. I promised to send a drawing, and he promised to ring me here to tell me whether it is the same person. He did not know why some clients received contracts in German and some in Italian."

Rachele had finished updating the diagram.

"You have done an excellent job. I'll ask my aunt Deborah to come and help you with the drawing. She can draw very well. She made the black and white drawing of the view from the Rialto meeting room. Did you discuss Fonda Trasporti?"

Carlo looked at his notes.

"I tried, but he told me he never reads the contracts. He only deals with the first two pages, which describe the purpose of the loan and the repayment terms, but only to check that the terms match the notes he sent to Zurich the previous week."

Dario took advantage of Rachele's silence.

"Do you think he told you the truth?"

"He didn't change his tone of voice. Either he rehearsed his answers very well, or he was telling the truth."

It was Dario's turn to take out his notepad.

"Enrico Fonda's sister, Annamaria, told me that as she was showing your brother out, two people arrived and told her they had a meeting with Enrico. They introduced themselves as Wilhelm and Johan and told her they knew the way. She wasn't sure who was who, but only the older one spoke with a heavy German accent. Those two saw Enrico Fonda alive after your brother. I have their description; it is vague. Maybe your brother can do better."

When Dario read from his notes, Carlo remarked that the description of the older one could match the Count von Falkenberg he knew. Rachele was more cautious.

"Let's ask Aunt Deborah to help you sketch Count Von Falkenberg's face. Once you are happy with it, I'll ask her to make copies and Dario will go back to Fonda Trasporti, hoping that Annamaria Fonda will recognise the man."

24 March 1930

Rachele was always very careful to separate the personal from the professional. She discussed work at home only when it was necessary. Although her parents, her brother Daniele, and his wife and their newborn child had been in Venice since Friday morning, she insisted on a meeting at the law firm on Monday. She could not tell who was more nervous. Her brother looked calm, but her father and uncle Viktor could not sit still.

Daniele had just finished describing his visit. Rachele stopped taking notes when he mentioned the two men who entered the premises as he was leaving.

"I had the impression that Annamaria Fonda had met the older blond gentleman several times. He introduced the younger man and said they had to talk to Enrico, who was waiting for them. She said to go right ahead, he knew the way."

Rachele took out her aunt's drawing of Graf von Falkenberg, which was made from Carlo Kovach's description.

"Was any name mentioned? "

Daniele shook his head. Rachele pushed the drawing towards her brother.

"Does this drawing look like the older of the two visitors?"

Daniele looked at the drawing for a few minutes.

"I think he looks like him. Who drew it?"

"Aunt Deborah, based on the description of Carlo Kovach. She was kind enough to make five copies. He is Graf Wilhelm von Falkenberg, a regular client of Pensione Vivaldi, where Carlo used to work. Somehow, he is connected with what happened."

Count Viktor Pesaro de Bonfili smiled for the first time.

"Deborah has always been a talented portrait painter, Daniele. She drew three portraits of you as a child and made the drawing of your bar mitzvah based on her memory of the synagogue in Trieste."

That comment brought the family back into the room, and

everybody relaxed. Rachele did not stop being 'Rachele, the lawyer'.

"Daniele, based on what you told me, there is a witness who can corroborate the time you left the company. The two of you are witnesses who can confirm when the other two men arrived at Fonda Trasporti. I'll write a letter to the police in Monfalcone, and next time you are summoned, I'll come with you."

Baron David Modiano's loud sigh of relief revealed his concern for his son. He looked at Count Viktor. They also had someone else in mind.

"What do we say to Franz Sedlak?"

Rachele was putting things away.

"The loan agreement mentions Fonda Trasporti, not Enrico Fonda. The company remains active, and the clause remains valid. Whether he should take the loan is another question, and it is for him to decide. The agreement is pretty standard other than that clause."

25 March 1930

Rachele's gut feeling was growing stronger and stronger. She believed that the "Fonda Trasporti" clause in the loan agreements, the ransacking of Wolfgang Meyer's room, the murder of Enrico Fonda, and Matteo Masiero's discovery there was gold in a locked bag were all connected. Things could get out of hand, and she might go over her discretionary amount of unbilled time. She organised a meeting with her boss, Franco Venier, one of the two partners of the law firm, to discuss the whole story and possibly request a temporary extension of her discretionary time, until they had reason to bill one or more of their clients.

Franco Venier listened carefully to Rachele's summary but still did not see the link.

"What makes you think everything is connected?"

Rachele expected that question.

"Well, some things add up only if they are, but I still miss evidence. I have compiled a list. There is the risk that I put the story together to confirm my gut feeling, but it is a risk I am prepared to run. Here it is. I tried to sort it logically rather than trying to create a timeline."

She passed the notepad to her boss, which was open on a page listing:

1) We know that Graf von Falkenberg vets all the lending agreements of the Milan office. Why are some contracts in German and some in Italian? Could that be a sort of code?

2) Wolfgang Meyer's room was ransacked, and we have found no evidence of anything missing. They could have taken something Herr Meyer did not want to admit he had. Could it be what was in the cubbyhole where the buzzer used to summon staff was located?

3) Matteo Masiero told us that sometimes, when he takes Herr Meyer to the station, he leaves a bag or a suitcase in his taxi with instructions to deliver it to Marghera. Recently, the bag had a hole, and he could see small gold bars. Could this be the ring of gold smuggling that Antonio Penzo was talking about?

4) Why is Fonda Trasporti in every contract?

5) Who killed Enrico Fonda and why? Is it connected with

Matteo Masiero delivering the bag to the Fonda Trasporti warehouse in Marghera?

6) What role does Graf von Falkenberg have in all of this? He is an eccentric German aristocrat who strives to be noticed. Why? Who is the younger man he introduced to Enrico Fonda the evening he was killed? Could it be the same man who collected the bag from Matteo Masiero, who thought little of his black balaclava, given how cold it was that day?

Rachele was watching her boss take his time reading the list. She was beginning to think her request for extra discretionary time would be denied. Then he adjusted his posture on the chair, picked up the notepad, and looked at her.

"I understand your gut feeling, and I think you should compare notes with Antonio Penzo. That list may be useful, and he may have something to add or explain to you. After all, he has talked to the police in Zurich."

Rachele took back the notepad her boss was offering her.

"I need to check, but I think Antonio Penzo is coming Friday morning to talk to me about the Gold smuggling."

Franco checked his diary.

"Yes, he has arranged to have lunch with me afterwards. We should start billing the courts for the time we spend with him, but we have some advantages in having him on our side. By the way, you can double your discretionary time for March and April with the provision that we may end up billing some or all of those hours if we find a client willing to pay."

She got what she wanted. Before she left the office, she invited him and his family for a meal after Passover.

Gabriele was in an excellent mood when he arrived at the law firm to walk home with his wife. Alvise was about to go home, but couldn't help but ask why his friend was so cheerful.

"Did you win the lottery?"

Gabriele laughed.

"Even better, we have finished all the meetings for the planning stage of the road bridge into Venice. Now we can talk about something else. For instance, how do you clear the area that will be the Venetian end of the bridge?"

Rachele had heard her husband's voice. She appeared ready to leave.

"I am ready. What are we celebrating?"

The two friends looked at each other.

"I have already told Alvise, I'll tell you on our way home."

The three left the law firm and started walking towards the Rialto Bridge, discussing the primary school in Campo San Polo Emma and Franco Cantoni would attend from the following October[i]. They decided to walk past the school together. They enjoyed each other's company. Alvise kept teasing his friend about his excellent mood with a conspiratorial tone because Rachele didn't know yet.

They parted company at Rio Tera Primo to go to their respective homes. Once they were alone, Gabriele turned to his wife.

"I know you were getting annoyed at the banter because you did not know what we discussed. I am going to reveal the secret of my excellent mood."

Rachele turned to him in mocking shock.

"At last. I wondered whether you had won a lottery and did not know how to tell me."

Gabriele told his wife the good news he had shared with his friend earlier. Rachele congratulated him and started teasing him about being bored at the office. When they reached Campo San Giacomo Dall'Orio, she turned serious.

"Do you think Venetian life will change? The mainland is getting closer."

Gabriele's reaction surprised her.

"You have turned into a Venetian! The mainland getting closer is a major concern for you."

Chapter Fourteen

March - April 1930

26 March 1930

When Anita walked into the kitchen, she did not expect to see Rachele clearing the table, and she could smell the cake in the oven.

"Isn't it getting a bit late to bake anything two weeks before we clean the kitchen for Passover?"

Rachele continued clearing the table. She did not even turn around.

"Good morning, Anita. I hope the back of my mind continued working while I was baking. I need to figure out how to prove a hunch. Also, I have faith that somebody will eat the chocolate cake in the oven by Sunday morning."

Anita was laying out the breakfast table while coffee was brewing.

"Would it help you talk about your hunch? Can you talk about it?"

Rachele thought about it as she put away the unused cake ingredients.

"I can only say that I am sure that three different things that happened to three clients are connected, but I have nothing to support it, or nothing yet."

Gabriele appeared in the kitchen with their daughters. The smell of the cake and coffee made him smile. He sat baby Diana in her high chair, Emma and Anna at the breakfast table, and put the bib over their nursery school overalls.

Anita was bringing the warm milk to the breakfast table when Rachele stopped washing up the utensils, clapped her hands, and shouted.

"I think I found a way. I hope Zia Deborah is available while Daniele is still in Venice."

Gabriele and Anita looked at each other. They were used to it. Gabriele was the first one to recover. He looked at Emma and Anna, whose faces showed some concern.

"Mum is all right. She must have had one of her hunches. Don't worry, we'll find out what she means in the next few days."

It turned out that Countess Pesaro De Bonfili was available and willing to help. Rachele, her brother, Daniele, and the Countess were in a meeting room. Rachele summarised why she asked them to meet her and what she hoped would happen that morning.

She passed a drawing of Graf Wilhelm von Falkenberg to her brother.

"This is a drawing of one of the two men who arrived at Fonda Trasporti as you were leaving."

Daniele interjected

"He is the older of the two, the one who had been there before and knew the way."

In her head, Rachele was beginning to think she had a chance to find evidence to prove her hunch.

"Exactly. What you just said is why I think everything is connected."

The countess couldn't help herself.

"He is the same man I saw at Pensione Vivaldi, the one who always dresses in white!"

Rachele smiled. So two people recognised Graf von Falkenberg. One of them placed him in Monfalcone the day Enrico Fonda was killed.

"Zia Deborah, you are here because I hope you can draw a sketch of the younger man that was with Graf von Falkenberg when they paid a visit to Enrico Fonda the day he died. Daniele is the only one who looked at him long enough. So, I'll leave you alone here. Let the receptionist know if you need anything. I have another meeting. I'll be back in about an hour. If you finish early, let the receptionist know."

Once she left the meeting room, the receptionist asked her if she was free to talk to Antonio Penzo, who was about to leave a message for her. Rachele told her to ask him if he could wait for her to go back to her office. He was.

When Rachele entered her office, her extension rang as she had expected.

"Judge Penzo, good afternoon. How are you? How can I help?"

"Franco, your boss, told me about your hunch. I have learnt to trust your hunches. I'll discuss the smuggling ring with my counterpart in Zurich in an hour, and I would like to hear your thoughts about our conversation. Are you available tomorrow morning?"

Rachele quickly checked her diary.

"If nobody has taken any appointment for me in the last hour, I am free from ten o'clock. I usually go home for lunch around twelve thirty."

"An hour will be enough. Unless I hear from you before 5 pm, I'll see you tomorrow morning at 11. Thank you. Till Tomorrow."

"Seeing you is always a pleasure, Judge Penzo. See you tomorrow."

Rachele sat down and thought about how different the professional relationship was now. Judge Antonio Penzo was now accustomed to women working as secretaries, assistants, and professionals. About eight years earlier, the man said she had 'a masculine brain.'

Before returning to her brother and aunt Deborah, Rachele left a message to Matteo Masiero at the taxi rank near Piazza San Marco. The message was a pretend query, leaving the law firm's number. It was a way to tell him she needed to see him.

A code they had agreed on when he signed up to be a client. She also told Carlo Kovach he needed to be in the meeting and to wait for Matteo Masiero to confirm his availability.

27 March 1930

Rachele arrived at the office in a good mood. Her morning had been great; nobody had woken up grumpy, and even Diana didn't scream when she woke up. She found her awake, looking at something on the ceiling, when she went to her room for the first feed of the day. She smiled when she saw her. The walk to work with Gabriele almost had a romantic atmosphere. As she was taking her coat off, she thought it had all the makings of a great day.

Matteo Masiero arrived at the time she requested. On her way to greet him, she walked past Carlo Kovach's desk, telling him to follow her. She asked a secretary to organise refreshments and bring them to one of the meeting rooms. After exchanging the required amount of small talk, she came to the point.

"I asked you here because I have to show you two sketches."

She pushed the drawing her aunt had made the previous day towards him.

"I appreciate you delivering the bag to somebody who disguises his face, but there is a brief description of the man under the image. Could this be him?"

Matteo Masiero studied the sketch and the description.

"The man I saw could be described in the same way. I think I recall blond hair peeking through the hat he wore once, but he usually wears a balaclava and always wears sunglasses. I can't say in all honesty, I recognise the face."

Then Carlo looked at the sketch.

"I don't think I ever saw him at the hotel. Count von Falkenberg meets people in our garden, but I wouldn't know because they don't have to come inside the hotel to access our café and the garden. Do you have a copy I can show around?"

Rachele pulled out another copy from the folder.

"I have five. Mr Masiero, I have another sketch to show you."

She pulled the sketch of Graf Wilhelm von Falkenberg out of the folder and pushed it in front of Matteo Masiero. He studied it and smiled.

"I picked this man at Pensione Vivaldi a few times. He speaks some Italian with a thick German accent. He always dresses in white."

"Thank you for your help. Do you mind looking at the other sketch one more time? I would like you to memorise the face and let me know if you see him. Please, do nothing else other than let me know."

He reassured her he would. Carlo left the meeting with a copy of the sketch of the younger man's face to find out if anybody at Pensione Vivaldi had seen him. Rachele showed her client out and went back to her office to wait for the judge.

Antonio Penzo was aware of Rachele's hunch, so the meeting started with her repeating the reasons behind it. However, when she finished, she also said she had some evidence to substantiate her hunch.

"My brother left when Enrico Fonda was still alive. He saw two men entering the premises as he was talking to Enrico Fonda's sister in the lobby. We have at least four people who recognised the older of the two men as a regular guest at Pensione Vivaldi, Count Wilhelm von Falkenberg, a German citizen living in Zurich. We also know that he decides who gets the contracts in German and who gets them in Italian. I am not sure it is relevant, but it might be."

Rachele pulled out the sketches of the two men and showed them to Judge Penzo.

"Yesterday, I asked my aunt, Countess Pesaro De Bonfili, to sketch the face of the younger man based on my brother's description. The Taxi driver did not recognise him because he had never seen his face. The person who receives the bag on the mainland either wears a balaclava or a hat and always wears sunglasses. However, he read Daniele's description and said it could be him."

Antonio Penzo looked at both sketches carefully. Asked if he could keep them, Rachele said she had another copy and one for the police. Then he told her his news.

"Two days ago, I received a phone call from a police inspector in Zurich. The same one that warned us of a gold-smuggling operation using Venice as a transit point. He informed me that the ringleader is a German citizen, based in Zurich, who travels to Venice frequently."

Rachele's face lit up.

"I am not thinking of Count Von Falkenberg. It is too early, and my hunch is not enough. But, Matteo Masiero, the taxi driver, came to tell me that someone had hidden two death threats in his taxi in a way that he could discover them only when he cleaned it at the end of his shift."

Rachele paused; she noticed her visitor was taking notes.

"Somebody who used his taxi must have hidden the notes. Matteo Masiero and the senior concierge at Pensione Vivaldi confirm that Count Von Falkenberg had used his taxi on both days."

Antonio Penzo saw it as an opportunity to tease 'his favourite lady lawyer'.

"This is as circumstantial as it can get; we need more evidence to act on your hunches."

Rachele recognised the light-hearted tone in the magistrate's voice and replied in an equally light-hearted tone.

"Although, in the past, you have acted on my gut feelings, and it turned out my guts were right."

Her visitor was about to drop a bombshell.

"This time, I have information that may justify your gut feeling, although it may not be considered evidence."

Rachele's face became serious. She took out her notepad. Antonio Penzo paused for effect.

"The Swiss police inspector told me that somebody we know is co-operating with the Police after he realised he was an accomplice of the Gold-smuggling ring, although he was acting in good faith. His lead witness is none other than Wolfgang Meyer."

Rachele almost stood up.

"I knew that there must have been a connection between those who ransacked his room and the Gold smuggling!"

The magistrate had one more revelation.

"Well, both Wolfgang Meyer and the Police Inspector will be in Venice in about ten days. The inspector asked me if he could use this office to meet Mr Meyer. After all, he is still a client of the law firm and may need to consult his lawyer. I cleared it with Franco, who told me to ask you."

Rachele felt she was about to prove her hunch.

"Only if I may show him the two sketches to see if he can identify them."

Antonio Penzo agreed. The professional meeting was over; they talked about Rachele's daughters for about ten minutes until Franco Venier came to take his friend to lunch, and Gabriele arrived to walk home with his wife.

03 April 1930

Rachele did not expect to receive a phone call from Zurich. The Police Inspector introduced himself and told her that Wolfgang Meyer had suggested he should call her. After the initial polite interaction, he came to the point.

"Wolfgang Meyer realised very early on that he was asked to take gold bars across the border. Better, he was blackmailed into taking gold bars across the border. He is helping us to stop this. He asked me to pass on to you the description of the man he refers to as his enforcer. Please let me know when you are ready to take notes."

Rachele couldn't help but think of a victory dance. This was further evidence that her gut feeling was pointing her in the right direction. She took out her notepad, positioned the phone headset between her head, tilted to the left, and her left shoulder.

"I am ready."

The Swiss Police inspector dictated the description. Halfway through, Rachele realised this might be the same person her brother had seen, the one they had nicknamed 'the younger blond'. When the Police Inspector had finished, Rachele read it back to him to make sure her notes were correct. Then she had a favour to ask.

"This description fits the person my brother saw enter the premises of Fonda Trasporti as he was leaving; it could be the last person to see Enrico Fonda alive..."

The Inspector could not resist

"or the person who killed him."

Rachele did not like interruptions, but this time she took it as the inspector finishing her sentences. She thought they would work well together.

"Can I ask you to organise a sketch artist and get a sketch of the enforcer's face based on Herr Mayer's description? I think it would be interesting to compare it with the drawing we made from my brother's description of the younger blond man."

The Police Inspector saw why the Italian judge had such a high opinion of this lady lawyer.

"Yes, I'll have it with me when I travel to Venice. I'll see you on Monday."

"I am looking forward to it. We'll show Herr Meyer our drawing and your drawing to my brother. If they both recognise the person, we'll be sure it is the same person. Do you know his name?"

Rachele couldn't see the inspector smiling; he could definitely work well with that woman.

"Unfortunately, I don't. Herr Meyer refers to him as the enforcer."

The conversation was over. After a couple of minutes of polite interaction, Rachele ended the call. She lifted her head and was surprised to find Carlo Kovach on the doorstep. He was clearly waiting for the end of the telephone conversation.

"Somebody at the Pensione Vivaldi café recognised the younger blond man."

Seeing Carlo Kovach gave Rachele an idea. She did not put away the notepad with the description.

"As my husband would say to me, please start from Chapter 1."

Carlo Kovack was too excited to detect the irony in her voice.

"I did not recognise the man your brother described as the younger of the two. I could not place him as a hotel guest or as someone who was a guest of Count von Falkenberg, but the café of Pensione Vivaldi has its entrance, and I showed the sketch to former colleagues who worked at the café. They recognised the face. No name yet, but we have three people who remember him sitting at one of the tables, talking to Count von Falkenberg."

Rachele took out another notepad.

"Did they name the count?"

"They just call him the eccentric German who always dresses in white."

Rachele was happy with that.

"I can think of at least four people who could testify that the description identifies Count Von Falkenberg. I have something to show you as well."

She passed Carlo the notepad with the description the Inspector had dictated.

"You speak German, don't you? This is a description a Swiss Police Inspector just shared with me. 'Do you recognise the person? By the way, you and Dario will meet the Inspector on Monday."

Carlo spent some time reading the description, closed his eyes for a short while, opened them, and smiled.

"I think it could also describe the younger blond man, the one whose face your aunt drew based on your brother's description."

Chapter Fifteen

April 1930

07 April 1930

Rachele was careful to use the part of the kitchen they had already cleaned for Passover. She was baking for the week when Jews cannot eat leavened bread, or much of the food they usually had throughout the year; only fruit and vegetables were safe from a complete reorganisation of the pantry.

Anita entered the kitchen, already dressed.

"Good morning, Rachele. Today, after I drop Emma and Anna at nursery school, I have promised Fiamma I will help to sort out the showroom for the first night Seder.[i]"

Rachele continued to prepare the cake; the two women were comfortable chatting with each other while working in the kitchen.

"Do you know how many people Fiamma and Samuele need to accommodate?"

Anita was busy preparing coffee without crossing the line between the part of the kitchen that had already been turned around and the one that hadn't yet.

"This year, it is only us, the Pesaro De Bonfilis, and the Mondanis. What are you baking?"

Rachele stopped mixing eggs and ground almonds.

"Only? That is a lot of people. What do we need to bring other than cakes and biscuits?"

"I'll find out this morning. Fiamma put together a menu yesterday, including who cooks what. Why are you baking this morning?"

"I am not tense. I know what we are supposed to do. We do not have that many days before Seder night, and I am behind."

They heard Diana cry. Rachele covered the bowl with the biscuit dough.

"Great timing, just when I can stop. I'll wash my hands and sort Diana out. Sorry for the mess, Anita."

The forthcoming big family night had monopolised the conversation on the walk to work. Once Rachele walked through the law firm's door, the receptionist told her that Antonio Penzo was already in the Rialto meeting room with another visitor. Rachele looked at her watch; the receptionist noticed and reassured her she was not late, but they were very early. She opened the door of the meeting room, told them she would be with them once she had dropped her coat and picked up what she needed for the meeting.

Ten minutes later, she was ready for them. She told the receptionist to tell Dario Zago and Carlo Kovach to join her as soon as possible, then entered the meeting room. Her two visitors stood up. Antonio Penzo made the introductions.

"Avvocato Modiano, this is Inspector Karl Schweitzer of the Swiss Police. He speaks Italian, but you should switch to German if you feel he has problems understanding Italian. Inspector Schweitzer, this is Avvocato Modiano, one of the most brilliant legal minds in Venice."

Rachele noticed the inspector did not offer his hand to shake, but bowed his head; an old-fashioned way to acknowledge the introduction.

"Thank you for the flattering introduction, Judge Penzo. Inspector Schweitzer, as the judge just said, feel free to switch to German if you think your Italian is not good enough."

She then sat down, wondering if the inspector might be Jewish by any chance. That would explain why he wouldn't shake her hand.[ii] She then opened a folder with the sketches and showed the inspector the sketch of the younger blond man as described by her brother, along with the portrait of Graf Wilhelm von Falkenberg.

"May I start with something that may or may not prove my theory? Based on our conversation last week, I wonder if this is the man Wolfgang Meyer calls 'the Enforcer'. He was seen entering the premises of Fonda Trasporti with Graf Von Falkenberg the day Enrico Fonda was killed."

Inspector Schweitzer reached for his briefcase, took out a folder, opened it, and put another drawing near the image of the young blond man.

"This drawing was based on Herr Mayer's description of the Enforcer. I think they could be the same person. What do you think?"

Both the magistrate and Rachele agreed that the two drawings could represent the same person. Judge Penzo smiled at Rachele, who nodded. The silent exchange was not lost on the Inspector.

"Judge Penzo already told me of your theory. I like it, but I agree it needs evidence to support it. Those two drawings are a beginning. We need more."

Rachele had an idea.

"I think I know how we can solve this problem. You mentioned that Wolfgang Meyer arrives tomorrow. Once a junior lawyer and the firm's researcher join us, I will share with you my idea for a plan so you and Judge Penzo could improve on it."

As if summoned, Dario Zago and Carlo Kovach entered the meeting room. As Rachele was making the introductions, Antonio Penzo thought that there would be very little to improve on her plan, based on her track record so far.

08 April 1930

Wolfgang Meyer loved being back in Venice, and the walk from Pensione Vivaldi to the law firm was long enough to enjoy the sunny but cold spring morning. He was eager to explain to Rachele why he had not mentioned that he was helping the Swiss police to bust a gold smuggling ring. His business still required a legal advisor in Italy, and he was satisfied with Rachele, so he did not want to risk losing her support. He arrived early and spent some time in a nearby café, people watching. When he saw Dario Zago walk towards the law firm carrying two binders, he took it as a signal that it was time to get up and face Avvocato Modiano.

The receptionist took him to one of the meeting rooms. She apologised on behalf of the law firm that he may have to wait a short while, not longer than fifteen minutes.

Rachele was not late; she was still explaining her idea to Karl Schweitzer, the Swiss Police Inspector, who was slowly but steadily joining the Avvocato Rachele Modiano Mendes admiration society. Carlo Kovach was also present. He had volunteered to help with some emergency translation when they had to inform the Italian Police, since Antonio Penzo had no German. Once they had all agreed on the plan's details, the three men and Dario Zago left for the meeting with the Italian Police. Dario Zago had been included at the last minute to ensure that the interests of their clients were protected. The Law Firm had four clients directly or indirectly involved with the story: Daniele Modiano (Rachele's brother), Matteo Masiero, Wolfgang Meyer, and Ascanio Moratti Limited.

Rachele entered the meeting room exactly fifteen minutes after the appointed time. Wolfgang Meyer turned around when he heard somebody was coming in. She noticed her client was nervous; he had not sat down since he arrived, although it was pretty obvious he had drunk the coffee.

"Herr Meyer, thank you for coming. I just finished talking with your acquaintance, Karl Schweitzer, who told me how much you have helped him."

Rachele had been very careful to sound as matter-of-fact as possible; she did not want to give the impression that she was mad or surprised that her client had not been entirely open to her. Wolfgang Meyer had arrived thinking of explaining to her why he did not share that he was helping the police in Zurich, so he replied to the question she had not asked.

"I am so sorry I did not share that with you. I did not know that Neue Zugkredit was indirectly involved. My company needs legal representation in Italy. I had never seen that loan contract before, then when the police in Monfalcone wanted to question me about the last hour of Enrico Fonda, I was so worried that I did not think of sharing any other information with you."

Rachele forced herself not to smile. She had to reassure her client.

"Herr Schweitzer explained to me he asked you not to tell anybody you were helping them, not even your wife. Usually, I expect my clients to be one hundred percent open with me, but in this case, I understand, I really do. I would need to tell you that this hour is part of the law firm's cooperation with the police, and therefore, it is not billed. If you need to discuss something else, I have to ask you to make another appointment."

Wolfgang Meyer relaxed. He stopped pacing the room, sat down, and asked if he could have some water. Rachele stood up and called the receptionist, asking her to bring water and two glasses. Once her client had finished drinking a full glass, she was ready to begin. She took out the sketch of the younger blond man.

"Herr Meyer, do you recognise this man?"

He looked at the sketch carefully.

"He is the person I call the Enforcer. I don't know his name. I think he is the one who broke into my room at Pensione Vivaldi the last time I was in Venice."

Rachele's reaction was a mixture of perplexity and satisfaction.

"Can you guess why he might have done that?"

Wolfgang Meyer took a piece of paper out of his pocket.

"They were looking for this. The phone number and code to contact Karl Schweitzer. I kept it in the cubbyhole where the maid's buzzer used to be. Luckily, I took it with me when I left for Trieste. I don't know why I did it:"

Rachele was smiling inside. She was adding more and more evidence to support her gut feeling.

"Do you think they suspected you were helping the police?"

Wolfgang Meyer was silent for a short while.

"I think they wanted to be reassured that I did not want to run away with the gold."

Rachele did not press the matter any further; it had become irrelevant.

"Herr Meyer, this is what we want you to do. Later this morning, Avvocato Zago and Carlo Kovach will speak with Matteo Masiero to ensure his cooperation. We know you told the Enforcer you are leaving for Trieste in two days. Here is what will happen..."

Once they had finished with the police, Carlo and Dario went to the taxi rank near San Marco to leave a message for Matteo Masiero. They were lucky he was there. So they explained to him what was going to happen when Wolfgang Meyer had booked him to go to the station two days later.

"You need to be here around nine am. A police officer will be here waiting for you; he will look young enough to be considered an apprentice or a helper and will dress accordingly. He will be there for your protection, but will not leave the cabin. You will follow your instructions as if nothing had happened, except you shall tell us the location where you have to deliver the bag, conveniently forgotten in your taxi by Wolfgang Meyer."

Matteo Masiero listened to the rest of the explanation, nodding whenever he thought the two young men wanted some reassurance that he had understood. In the end, he only had two questions.

"How will I recognise the policeman? Will he have a gun?"

Chapter Sixteen

April 1930

10 April 1930

Rachele and Anita were both up early. One was baking the last batch of biscuits for the family's Passover meal, while the other was putting away things that wouldn't be used until after Passover.[i] Anita had her head inside a cupboard, cleaning it.

"Rachele, if you can think of anything we have to buy for the Passover week, please add it to the list. Fiamma and I go shopping when the girls are at nursery. Sofia has volunteered to babysit for Diana."

"I assume you did not have a hard time convincing her to do it."

Anita had finished cleaning the cupboard and was now taking the Passover plates from their box and putting them in the clean cupboard.

"Sofia volunteered after Fiamma told her we were planning a pre-Passover shopping trip."

Anita realised Rachele had not reacted to what she had just said. She turned around and realised that her close friend and employer was staring at the finished batch of biscuits.

"Are you all right?"

Anita's voice brought Rachele back to reality.

"I am fine. I was just thinking of what is supposed to happen today. I know I said I would be in the office at 10 this morning, but I'm wondering if the plan we put together will work. The reputation of my guts depends on it."

Matteo Masiero noticed a young man walking along the pier of the Taxi rank near Piazza San Marco. When the young man approached his speedboat, he pointed him to the front of the queue, thinking he needed a taxi. The young man was not a prospective client.

"If you are Matteo Masiero, I am your new apprentice."

He took out a Police ID card from his right pocket.

Matteo noticed the bulge in his right pocket. He took the ID and checked it.

"I am Matteo Masiero. May I call you Bepi? Are you sure your birthdate is correct? You do not look a day over 18 to me."

The young man smiled.

"That is why I am usually chosen for this sort of undercover work."

Bepi hopped on the speedboat and went inside the cabin. Matteo gave him a book.

"If you are an apprentice on his first day at work, you would usually start by studying the rules for maritime traffic inside the lagoon. When we meet our passengers, you sit inside and pretend to study."

The young man did as he was told. After about twenty minutes, Matteo started the engine, cast off the moorings, and left for Pensione Vivaldi to fetch Wolfgang Meyer.

Rachele was about to start a meeting with two clients who had agreed to seek her advice on a dispute before going to court. She bumped into Dario Zago, who was about to leave the firm for the station to meet Rachele's brother.

"Please tell Daniele that he has nothing to worry about. He is here because he is the only one who could establish whether the enforcer and the young blond man he saw at Fonda Trasporti are the same person."

"I have to hurry. We do not want to risk being seen by the wrong people. We have arranged to meet the police at a side entrance."

Rachele felt she had to remind Dario he was only a trainee lawyer.

"It should not be necessary, but if you think there is a need for experienced legal advice, call the firm. If I am still busy, we shall send you somebody available."

Dario thought Rachele was nervous and was turning into a mother. He just smiled, told her not to worry, and left for the station. Rachele took a deep breath and entered the meeting room. She hated having to arbitrate between two clients.

"Sorry to keep you waiting. Before we start, I need to ask both of you to read carefully and sign these documents, stating that you will abide by my decision and not go to court on this matter for at least six months unless some new evidence emerges."

~

Karl Schweitzer was in Wolfgang Meyer's room to go through what was supposed to happen.

"Officially, you are supposed to leave for Trieste to visit a client and come back to Venice tomorrow. As you know, you are not going anywhere. We shall put you up in a different hotel tonight if necessary. You meet your solicitor and a police officer at the station, and you will be brought to the Questura to be available as a witness. We need an official identification of the enforcer."

They arrived in the lobby separately, a few minutes before the taxi arrived. As they were about to leave, Graf von Falkenberg appeared, asking Wolfgang Meyer if he minded taking his visitor to the station as well. He would leave half the fare with the concierge.

Wolfgang Meyer did not know how to tell Karl Schweitzer that the 'visitor' was, in reality, the enforcer. He felt he could not say no. Matteo Masiero thought that the young man could be the person he saw wearing a balaclava and black clothes. He had a quick word with Bepi, the plainclothes policeman, who just pointed to his right pocket, almost tapping on his gun.

When the two men boarded with the luggage, Matteo greeted them and felt he had to introduce the young man who was with him in the boat.

"This is Bepi. He just started his apprenticeship as a future taxi driver. He needs to study the manual first. If you need to have a confidential conversation, he'll come and sit next to me."

The two men made polite noises but told him they had just met, so it was unlikely they had anything confidential to talk about.

Bepi cast off the mooring, and the taxi left Pensione Vivaldi's private pier.

Karl Schweitzer did not know he would meet the eccentric middle-aged blond man again before the end of the day.

When they arrived at the station, the enforcer made no move to get off. Wolfgang Meyer disembarked, leaving one piece of luggage in the taxi. He walked inside, got on the first coach of the train to Trieste, where he met with Dario Zago and a policeman. They were supposed to get off at Mestre station, on the other side of the bridge, where they would take a train back to Venice and leave the station via a side entrance.

Meanwhile, the young blond man simply said.

"I am staying on board and going with you where you have to deliver this bag."

Now that Matteo heard the man's voice, he thought he was the man wearing a balaclava. He looked at Bepi, who put his hand outside his right-hand pocket and smiled.

 Herr Meyer had recognised the enforcer; he saw through a slightly different appearance, thanks to the longer hair kept in place by pomade. It was not part of the plan outlined in the note that came with the bag he retrieved from the left-luggage counter in Venice a couple of days earlier. So, when he got on the train, he shared his concern with Dario Zago and the policeman, who thought they'd better forget about their trip up and down the railway bridge. The policeman noticed the conductor. He stopped him, showed him his badge, and asked for his help to leave the train as inconspicuously as possible. The conductor led them to the luggage and freight coach, stopped a member of the station staff, and asked him to let the three men through the staff subway to platform 1, where the police station was. Once they were in the goods lift to access the staff subway, the policeman took out his ID and explained that they needed to take extra precautions in case someone was watching to ensure they got on the train and stayed there.

Meanwhile, on board Matteo Masiero's water taxi, nobody was talking. The plainclothes policeman tried to look as concerned as a young teenager on his first day of apprenticeship would be. The Enforcer had a slight variation of the plan.

"Somebody else needs to come on board. Could you please return to Rialto? We will be late, but they will wait for us."

Matteo just nodded. Again, the policeman put his hand just outside the right pocket. He meant it as a reassurance gesture, but Matteo was not reassured.

When Karl Schweitzer heard of the change of plans, he was not happy. They often meant trouble. However, he reacted quickly and suggested they take Wolfgang Meyer back to the Venier-Zanin law firm, where he would wait until they needed him as a witness. They would send an unmarked police speedboat.

Meanwhile, Pensione Vivaldi's concierge rang the law firm, asking to speak to Carlo Kovach. Rachele was in the lobby; the arbitration session had just finished. She took the call from the receptionist's counter.

"I am not sure whether it matters, but just in case it does, Count von Falkenberg checked out three days before his expected departure day. He declined my offer to call him a taxi and told me that a friend was waiting for him at the taxi pier near Rialto."

Carlo's former colleague would have been amused if he could have seen her reaction. The receptionist later told a colleague that she almost turned into an animal that had seen its prey and was ready to sprint.

"I think it does matter. Thank you, thank you. I need to go now, sorry to be so brusque. All the best."

She called Antonio Penzo. When the magistrate replied, she apologised for the hurry, but she had to call a client as soon as possible. She told him about the count. Judge Penzo asked her to repeat it to Karl Schweitzer.

After they hung up, the two men looked at each other. The Venetian in Antonio Penzo allowed him to calculate the approximate time required to walk from Pensione Vivaldi to the taxi pier near Rialto. He remembered that one of his aunts had a jewellery shop nearby. He rang her and explained that he needed her help. She should ring him when she sees a tall blond man dressed in white, with a large bag or a suitcase. He thought it would take ten to fifteen minutes to walk to the taxi rank. His aunt heard the urgency in his voice and told him she would stand by the shop's door and call him as soon as she saw that man.

Dario Zago had the idea of reaching the law firm from the back. They were all thinking of taking extra precautions because nobody knew how many people were involved in smuggling gold bars through Venice. He told the driver to go to Rio Della Fava. Once they were almost in sight of the Rialto Bridge, the police driver turned left. Dario instructed him to turn right at the next corner and leave them at the first available mooring.

He told the policeman who was with them that Calle de l'Aquila Nera was at the other end of the sottoportego, and he knew a way to reach the Law Firm without using the front door. They walked along the Calle until they reached a leather goods shop. Dario took them inside, greeted the owner, and told him they needed to access his office without being seen. The policeman was surprised that the shop owner greeted Dario and did not react to his request. He took a set of keys out of a drawer near the cash register and led them through the back of the shop to a locked door. He opened it and kept it open for them. Dario thanked him. Once they were in the courtyard, Dario explained they used this route whenever they needed a 'confidential access' to the law firm. They walked across a tiny courtyard to a covered porch. Dario took them through three sets of doors, and then they arrived at the stairwell leading to the office. Once they were inside, the policeman left, and Dario left Herr Mayer in one of the meeting rooms where he was supposed to wait until Antonio Penzo or Karl Schweitzer rang Rachele to tell her they had caught the Enforcer and possibly others.

Judge Penzo's aunt did not have to wait long. She noticed a middle-aged blond man, all dressed in white, approach the pier with the taxis carrying a medium-sized leather suitcase. She saw a speedboat approaching with one passenger on board: a blond man in his late twenties or early thirties. The man dressed in white was waiting for them. The young man sitting next to the driver caught the suitcase. She noticed the driver talking to his passengers, then he got off the boat, passed an envelope to another taxi driver, got on again, and they left. She immediately called her nephew and described what she had seen.

Antonio Penzo shared the description of the man with Karl Schweitzer. He also added that once again, Avvocato Modiano's guts may prove correct. He was glad that they were on the same side this time as well.

Meanwhile, at the Venier-Zanin law firm, the receptionist received a call from a taxi driver attempting to reach Avvocato Modiano on behalf of Matteo Masiero. She thought it was urgent enough to put it through immediately. The caller told Rachele that he had received an envelope with her business card inside, and Matteo instructed him to say to her "Punta San Giuliano," but he did not know what it meant. Rachele thanked him and told him that the message was clear to her. She knew what she had to do.

She immediately called Antonio Penzo.

"I just had a message on behalf of Matteo Masiero. We had agreed on a system to tell me if something was not going according to plan. They are heading for Punta San Giuliano from Rialto."

Rachele's efficiency did not surprise the magistrate; he could not explain the change of plan.

"Why change from the Austrian fort?"

Rachele shook her head. Without thinking, she was on the phone, and the judge could not see her.

"I don't know. Can you check if there is any ship sailing from Marghera later today or tomorrow?"

"Let me check. I'll let you know as soon as I know."

After Judge Penzo hung up, he contacted the police station at the port and asked for help. He also called the Carabinieri[ii] station near the Austrian fort. He asked for their help in informing the police officers waiting at the Austrian fort they had to proceed to the commercial port in Marghera. Another phone call confirmed that there were four ships due to sail within the next 24 hours. He rang the police station at the commercial port and asked them to have men near each one of those ships, just in case. Then they had to wait for events. Karl Schweitzer used the other phone on the desk to contact Rachele.

Meanwhile, in the lagoon, Matteo Masiero thought he needed more time for the police to react to his message. He had an idea that might just buy them time and hoped his passengers had no experience with speedboats. Bepi, the plainclothes policeman, was Venetian, or at least from the Veneto region, so he whispered to him in Venetian dialect.

"Please follow my lead and do not contradict me."

He slowed the engine, then left Bepi at the helm and went to speak to his passengers.

"There is a problem with oil in the engine. I have to slow down, otherwise we risk not reaching Punta San Giuliano."

The older of his two passengers was not happy, but shrugged his shoulders and simply said.

"It happens. It shouldn't be a problem as long as we can reach our destination reasonably early."

Matteo was ready for that.

"Yes, the light is not blinking, so there is no risk we get stuck in the lagoon. It is just prudent to slow down."

The younger man did not take it as graciously as his fellow passenger.

"Show me the red light. I have a gun. I'll use it if you play tricks on us."

He went to the front of the water taxi, and when Matteo appeared, Bepi stepped aside as any young apprentice would do. He had heard the conversation and put his hand in his right pocket. Holding his gun somehow reassured him.

Matteo Masiero was very calm. He took the helm and pointed to the red light on the dashboard.

"You see, it is not flashing yet, so we can keep going. We just have to slow down."

He also hoped that somebody would notice a speedboat moving slowly in the lagoon. Venetian water taxi drivers were famous for loving to push their speedboats as fast as they could whenever they could.

The younger blond man did not return to his previous seat while the boat slowed down. He stayed where Matteo was, a hand in his jacket pocket. Bepi assumed he had a gun there and made a point of not losing sight of that hand.

When they were near the pier smaller boats used at Punta San Giuliano, Matteo noticed a police speedboat. When they were within earshot, he stopped the engine and shouted.

"I have a problem with the engine. Can you come and help?"

The younger blond man was not happy about that. Bepi hoped he sounded convincing.

"Occasionally, a police boat helps other boats in distress. Mr Masiero probably thinks it is better if we are towed to the pier. I think he will get the engine checked. There are mechanics at the port."

Matteo was pleased that the plainclothes policeman was smart enough to intervene and defuse the situation. The police speedboat reached them, and somebody threw a rope. Bepi sprang up and tied it to the bow of the boat. He also told the police to wait until he was back with an oar. After a conversation in Venetian dialect between Matteo, the 'ship's captain', and the senior police officer on board the speedboat, the police threw a rope for Matteo. Bepi had found the oar, put it aside, and tied the rope. Towing could start.

There were policemen near the four ships that were due to sail in the following twenty-four hours. They were trying to be as inconspicuous as possible. The head of the police station at the port had requested help from Customs Officers; after all, it was suspected to be a smuggling ring. There were two customs officers on board each of the four ships, ostensibly to inspect something a colleague had forgotten to check a few hours earlier. The two men approached a cargo heading for Portugal. As they had already stepped onto the gangway, four policemen came out and shouted for them to stop. The two Customs

Officers who were on board the ship blocked the ship's end of the gangway.

Graf von Falkenberg and his enforcer had nowhere to go. They were still at the pier end of the gangway. If they threw the bag with the gold, it would have hit the pier, not the water.

11 April 1930

Rachele thought that the walk to work with Gabriele was the lull before the storm. Today was not just a Friday, it was the day when her brother would identify the younger man who had been arrested at Marghera the day before. It was also the eve of Passover, and she wanted to help prepare for the big extended family dinner that evening and help Anita sort out the food for the smaller dinner at their home the following evening. Her sister-in-law, Daniele's wife, had arrived from Trieste to spend the first two days of Pesach with her husband and the whole Mendes clan. Daniele Modiano would not have arrived home in time for the holiday, so his wife joined him for the entire weekend. They would go back to Trieste on Monday morning.

Work, family, and the forthcoming holiday were fighting for attention in Rachele's mind. She barely listened to what her husband was saying. There was something that was still nagging her. She was happy her hunch had proven right yet again, but she was sure she had overlooked something. When they were walking by the Rialto fish market, Gabriele drew her attention to a colony of seagulls waiting for discarded fish. Rachele's reaction surprised him.

"Yes! Graf von Falkenberg could not have witnessed Wolfgang Meyer's arrival in Venice if he were in Monfalcone. I must make sure Daniele has the opportunity to identify him as well!"

Gabriele looked at his wife.

"This is not even chapter 4. Care to give me a summary from the beginning, if you may talk about it?"

Rachele smiled, thought about it for a few seconds.

"You mentioned seagulls that led me to another bird, a falcon. Falkenberg means Falcon mountain. Believe it or not, you provided the last piece of the puzzle that I needed to complete the picture. He insisted on writing an affidavit to establish he was at Pensione Vivaldi, not in Monfalcone."

Once she was at her desk, she called Antonio Penzo to share what she had figured out. They should ensure that Daniele has the opportunity to identify Count von Falkenberg as the older, blond man he saw entering the premises of Fonda Trasporti as he was leaving.

Antonio Penzo took the chance of asking for a favour.

"Once again, your hunch was spot on. I will always follow your gut feelings! I have a favour to ask. It turns out Karl Schweitzer is Jewish, and he is stuck in Venice until at least Wednesday next week."

Rachele interrupted the judge.

"He is welcome to join us for all meals. Tonight at my in-laws, tomorrow at our place, the rest of the time we'll see. Tell him we shall feed him until he has to go back to Zurich."

Epilogue

April 1930

15 April 1930

By the third day of Passover, Karl Schweitzer had gone past the unease of a last-minute guest. He was slowly becoming familiar with the whole Mendes/Pesaro De Bonfili/Modiano clan. On the fourth night, the clan was having dinner at the Pesaro De Bonfilis, a new Venetian household for him.

Gabriele and Rachele met Karl Schweitzer at the beginning of Strada Nova. It was easier than trying to explain to him how to get to the Pesaro De Bonfili residence. On the way to their uncle and aunt's home, they tried to prepare their new friend.

"This will be your first evening in a Venetian Grand House. During Passover, we have meals in what is usually a large sitting room. It faces the Grand Canal. Also, half the objects you see around the house could easily be found in a museum."

Rachele added

"I act as if I am used to them, but I am not, and I have known them all my life."

Karl Schweitzer did not comment. He simply thanked them for their warning. However, once inside, he was genuinely surprised by the art casually displayed and the Art déco furniture. Gabriele and Rachele noticed he did not move for a few seconds after entering the room where they were going to have dinner.

During the meal, the conversation flowed. After all, half the people around the table spoke German. Baron Davide and Count Viktor were the first to break the social conversation with a direct question; they asked if she had figured out the reason behind the clause concerning Fonda Trasporti. Rachele looked at Karl Schweitzer, who smiled and nodded; he realised that information was the price he had to pay for being hosted for meals during the rest of his stay in Venice. The nod was his silent agreement to be involved in the conversation. Rachele felt she could start from the beginning.

"It was part of a plan to smuggle gold out of Switzerland. I think Herr Schweitzer can explain it better from the beginning."

Karl Schweitzer put the knife and fork down and looked at the rest of his lemon sole for a few seconds.

"It all started when a senior executive of a Swiss Bank, a German-born aristocrat, noticed that there were accounts held by Russians who had been dormant since before the beginning of the war. He reckoned that ten years after the October revolution in Russia, those who had not made it out were dead or stuck forever in the Soviet Union."

Countess Deborah took a sip of wine and put down the glass.

"How could he get access to that money?"

Rachele smiled, hoping Karl Schweitzer didn't mind being interrupted. He was too polite to show irritation or had no problem with interruption.

"He created an account in the name of a company he controlled. He found somebody who could counterfeit signatures based on the ones deposited with the bank. Once he had that, it was easy to create letters requesting the transfer of funds to his company's account. Those funds were used to buy gold. He now had to solve three other problems: (1) How to take the gold out of the country, (2) which country was the final destination, and (3) what did he have to do to smuggle the gold there, or somewhere where it could easily be sold whenever he needed cash."

Karl then looked at Rachele, who felt it was her turn to continue.

"Graf von Falkenberg had clients with very shaky financial histories. One of them was the company owned by Wolfgang Meyer's father-in-law. So he paid the company loan in exchange for Herr Mayer's help. Herr Meyer took regular business trips to Venice. He was perfect to take the Gold out of Switzerland."

Rachele nodded to Karl Schweitzer, who continued.

"Graf von Falkenberg did not know that Herr Meyer came to us almost immediately. We asked him to follow the count's directions and keep us informed. However, he did not know the role of Fonda Trasporti or anybody else involved in the scheme except for one young man, whom he called the Enforcer, who was the one who discussed with him the day he would have had to organise the delivery of the gold."

Baron Davide Modiano and Count Viktor were among the clients who visited the law firm to seek an opinion on the loan contract, specifically regarding the 'Fonda Clause'.

"What was the role of Fonda Trasporti in all of this?"

Karl Schweitzer and Rachele looked at each other. She had the answers.

"According to what the police had established, all contracts had the 'Fonda Clause', but it applied to the contracts that were delivered to the client in German. Fonda Trasporti was supposed to carry the Gold to another port whenever it was difficult to use Venice. Also, their office at Marghera was providing the logistics."

Count Viktor was not convinced.

"But why did they agree to do it?"

Rachele smiled at her uncle.

"Graf von Falkenberg used part of the money he had embezzled from dormant accounts to pay their loan."

Rachele's mother had a question.

"How did Daniele become involved in all of this?"

Again, Rachele felt she had to let Karl Schweitzer eat his fish and vegetables. So she replied.

"Daniele ended up being very important to secure the arrest of Graf von Falkenberg and his enforcer. As you know, he is a very close friend of Franz Sedlak, who was helped by dad and uncle Viktor to try to save his family's shipyard. So, he decided to take a look at Fonda Trasporti and ask a few questions. He arrived just as Wolfgang Meyer was leaving; therefore, he could testify that he spoke to Enrico Fonda after Herr Meyer left."

Rachele noticed that Karl Schweitzer had stopped eating; she thought he was getting ready to continue at the right moment. He nodded, Rachele took it as a sign she should continue.

"His meeting with Enrico Fonda was pleasant but a bit inconclusive; he was vague. As Enrico Fonda's sister was showing him out, Graf von Falkenberg and the enforcer arrived. Daniele and Annamaria Fonda were still talking when Graf von Falkenberg left, leaving the enforcer. Annamaria Fonda told Daniele that she thought the meeting would be very tense, given what her brother had told her that morning."

Karl Schweitzer put down his knife and fork, a sign he was ready to continue.

"She also told the police that her brother wanted to agree on a time when their arrangement would expire. After all their four years' loan only had eighteen months to go when Graf Von Falkenberg paid it on his behalf."

He apologised to Rachele, who finished answering her mother.

"Daniele identified Graf Von Falkenberg and the Enforcer. Annamaria Fonda also stated the count spent less than ten minutes in Enrico Fonda's office, but the Enforcer stayed for an hour. Annamaria Fonda went home. An hour later, she and her sister-in-law went back because they hadn't heard from Enrico. That's when they found the body."

Esther Modiano smiled with maternal pride.

"Daniele established the link."

Karl Schweitzer felt he had to intervene.

"Your son gave the police the reason to check the Enforcer's fingerprint, and they matched. Without his statement, we would have taken them back to Switzerland. They may not have ever found the person whose fingerprint matched some they found at the scene. The murderer of Enrico Fonda would not have been found."

The Countess felt she had to intervene.

"Now, can we all leave Rachele and our guest alone so they can finish their dinner. We have amazing cakes baked by Rachele, and we can't have them until they have finished."

16 April 1930

Antonio Penzo and Rachele were at the station with Karl Schweitzer, who was going back to Zurich alone. Graf von Falkenberg and the Enforcer had been arrested for the murder of Enrico Fonda. Switzerland could apply for their extradition once they had served their sentence in Italy.

The Swiss Police Inspector thanked Antonio Penzo for his professional help and then turned to Rachele.

"I enjoyed sharing meals with your extended family for the past few days. Your boss has put me in touch with a friend of yours, Alvise Cantoni. He helped me organise flowers for you, your mother-in-law, and Countess Pesaro De Bonfili as a small token of my gratitude. I am looking forward to spending the last two days of the holiday with my family."

After the train left, Antonio Penzo and Rachele walked towards the waterbus stop to return to their respective offices. The judge turned to Rachele.

"Please tell me, how do you do it?"

"How do I do what?"

Silvano Stagni

"This is the umpteenth time you convince everybody to follow your gut feeling, and it is the umpteenth time your guts were right."

Rachele Modiano Mendes

I shamelessly borrowed from my mother's family to create the series, the Mendeses, the Modianos, and other fixed characters. My maternal grandmother's family was the inspiration for the Modianos, a family made of very strong characters who were all very close and got along very well; or, at least, if they didn't, they kept it to themselves and showed a united front to their children and grandchildren.

My maternal grandmother was the inspiration for Rachele Modiano Mendes. I hope I managed to convey her strong character, empathy, and unconditional love for her family and close friends who had become part of her family.

In Italy, women do not change their names. In the old paper identity cards, where men had 'married', women had the last name of their husbands. Rachele had two legal signatures: Rachele Modiano, and Rachele Modiano Mendes. She could be introduced as Mrs Modiano Mendes, or Mrs Mendes. Professionally, she would be 'Avvocato Modiano' (Avvocato is lawyer in Italian, and it is also used as a title, like Doctor in the

Anglo-Saxon World) because she was not married when she graduated.

It was uncommon for women born in 1897 to attend University, but the real-life Rachele did. My grandmother always refused "to be a handbag in her husband's arms", as she used to say to anybody who asked. She would also add that she was lucky to have a supportive husband and working environment, something not at all common in pre-WWII Italy.

Venice street names

Venice is one of the characters in the book. The characters in the story walk around Venice, and their route is often described in detail.

Venice streets and squares have unusual names. There is only one '**Piazza**' (Square in Italian), Piazza San Marco. All the others are called **Campo** (Field in Italian), or, if they are small, **Campiello**. Streets are not called Via (Street in Italian), but **Calle**, **Ruga**, and sometimes even **Sottoportego** if they are under arches or start after an arch.

Sidewalks on a canal can be called **Riva** (usually where boats could moor) or **Fondamenta**.

Salizada is a slightly larger alleyway, sometimes referred to as one of the earliest paved roads in Venice. Salizadas often curve, just like most canals, so it is likely that they were canals or ditches filled in to create a road.

Rio Tera is a street that resulted from a canal being filled with earth in the past. There are over forty streets in Venice that were once canals. Most of them were filled in the nineteenth century. The most recent was filled in 1915, while the oldest was filled in 1774.

There are a few exceptions. Two results are from projects initiated when Venice was part of the Austrian Empire (between 1815 and 1870), and one occurred during Fascist Italy.

'Strada' in Italian means 'big road' – **Strada Nova** (new big road). Once the railway arrived in Venice in the 1830s, there was a need for a way to walk from the station to the Rialto area. The Austrians filled in narrow canals and demolished a few houses, resulting in the creation of Strada Nova.

Via – There is only one 'Via' in Venice, called **Via Garibaldi**. It used to be a major canal, but the Austrian rulers decided to cover it up and create a wide road with outdoor cafés, similar to those found in Vienna.

Piazzale in Italian is a large open square. When the fascist regime built a road bridge into Venice alongside the Austrian-built railway bridge, they demolished an area to create a bus terminal and multi-level parking, the area is called **Piazzale Roma**. It is now the connection between Venice and the ordinary world of roads, buses, cars, taxis, and so on.

Historical Notes

The railway bridge was built in 1846, when the Austro-Hungarian empire ruled Venice. The road bridge next to it (nowadays called Ponte della Libertà) was opened in 1933, the final design was approved in 1932. I have taken the liberty of assuming that they had started working out what they had to do to prepare the Venetian end of the bridge in 1930. Gabriele Mendes is a civil servant in charge of permits for any work involving canal side building and canals.

Acknowledgments

I'll never tire of repeating it. Writing may be a solitary endeavour but it takes a village to create a book. Let me start by thanking my beta readers Rose Kemps, Andrea Rosen, Patricia Lane, Daniella Pinkstein, Deborah Drake, and Dan Sonnet. Their feedback has been invaluable. You owe it to them if you do not fall asleep reading this book!

Deborah Drake and Rose Kemp also provided valuable feedback and encouragement throughout the writing and revision process of this book. Katryn Koromilas is a dear friend who provides support in a subtle yet meaningful way; her messages are always a source of encouragement.

London Writers' Salon supported the discipline of writing every day. It is incredible what four fifty-minute writing sessions a day of writing 'alone but together' on a silent Zoom call can achieve.

I will always be grateful to Tracey Bickley who a few years ago gave me the push to continue writing my first book, and to Kimberlee Walker who was the first to tell me about 'having coffee with my characters'; it is a great way to create multi-dimensional profiles of the fictitious people who populate my stories. I have learnt a lot about them during those 'coffee and cake' sessions.

I would also like to thank Enrico Moscatelli, an Italian lawyer based in Genoa, for all the legal questions I have been asking him as I write.. Rachele Modiano Mendes is a lawyer inspired by my grandmother, but she hasn't been around for over thirty years and cannot answer hypothetical questions on Italian law. Thankfully, Enrico can.

Family and friends provided encouragement, listened (or acted as if they listened) when I let off steam, when I bragged, and when I bored them. Thank you, Alessandra, Alessandro, Maria Vittoria, David, Michelle, Eyal, Moshe, Jonathan, Sam, and Rose.

I am also grateful to the librarian of the Biblioteca Marciana in Venice, my invaluable source of information for anything about Venice, who bears with me whenever I asked bizarre question, like "Where can I find information about the industrial past of Giudecca Island?" or "Do you have an hotel directory from 1930? I need to see what amenities hotels were advertising."

Last but not least, thank you Venice. It is a city vilified by over-tourism, but the magic is still there. If you move away from Instagram locations and the hordes of visitors, you can still find magical corners. Writing stories that take place in Venice takes me back there and make me relive the magic from the comfort of my home in London, by the river Thames.

About the Author

Silvano Stagni is a multilingual citizen of the world, a father of four, and a cosmopolitan character with a long and varied life. In his youth, he was blessed to have many storytellers, people from different cultures and walks of life. He heard stories from the Imperial Court in Vienna, stories from the Kenyan bush, stories of seafarers, stories of survivors, and stories of fighters. He started writing articles, white papers, and opinion pieces during his previous professional life as an expert in the implementation of financial regulations. Now it is his turn to tell stories.

You can find more stories on his Substack https://authorsilvano.substack.com/

Notes

Chapter 1

i. Avvocato means lawyer in Italian. It is used as a formal title, like Doctor in English. Emma was being very polite and formal. She knew she was talking to her mother's boss, a grown-up who was not part of the family.

Chapter 2

i. A town near Trieste, a port on the other side of the Adriatic Sea from Venice, where Rachele was born and where her family lives.
ii. In Italy it is the equivalent of passing the bar exam.

Chapter 4

i. Venetians who live in the historic city in the lagoon call themselves 'Venesian de aqua' (lit. Venetian of the water) to differentiate from those who live in Mestre, mainland Venice, who are 'Venesian de tera' (Venetian of the land).
ii. Literally 'Madame Lawyer', in formal German.

Chapter 7

i. The word for fog in Venetian dialect. It is also used to indicate the atmosphere created by light fog, where everything is still visible but looks slightly out of focus.

Chapter 8

i. The German names for Trieste and Gorizia. Those two cities had been part of the Kingdom of Italy since 1918. Before the end of World War I they were part of the Austrian Empire.

Chapter 9

i. In Italy, 'Avvocato' (Lawyer) is also used as a title, like 'doctor' in English.

It is the formal way of introducing yourself to a stranger in a professional conversation.

Chapter 11

i. In formal German, you use as many titles as possible. Wolfgang Meyer would have said Herr Richter Penzo, even if Antonio Penzo was a relatively junior judge.

ii. It is not part of the Sephardi tradition to have the marrying couple fast 24 hours before the wedding like Ashkenazi Jews do. The Mendes Clan is Sephardi.

iii. One of the synagogues in the Venetian ghetto.

Chapter 12

i. During the Jewish Holiday of Purim, the story of Esther is read twice, either in synagogue or at home. She was the favourite wife of the Persian King Ashverosh; she saved the Jews from being slaughtered. This is a holiday often called 'the Jewish Carnival'. Gabriele and Rachele discuss the logistics for a children's party in the afternoon. Strictly speaking, Purim is not a religious holiday, so even observant Jews like Gabriele and Rachele can work if needed.

Chapter 13

i. In Italy, October 1st used to be the beginning of the school year.

Chapter 15

i. Seder (lit. order) is the name of the traditional Passover meal that includes the tale of the Jews' escape from slavery in Egypt, and the crossing of the Red Sea (when the water parted)

ii. Traditional orthodox Jewish men do not shake a woman's hand, just in case they might break one of the rules regulating contact between men and women.

Chapter 16

i. In the diaspora, Passover lasts eight days, calculated from sunset to sunset, and only the first two and the last two are considered holidays. During those eight days, traditional Jews do not use the same kitchen utensils, crockery, and cutlery they use the rest of the year, and the 'usual stuff' is put away.

ii. The Carabinieri are Italy's national gendarmerie, a military police force with a dual role of both military and civil police duties.

9 781068 611155